ALSO BY BRIAN DRAKE

VENGEANCE STRIKE

SAM RAVEN
BOOK EIGHT

BRIAN DRAKE

**ROUGH
EDGES
PRESS**

Vengeance Strike
Paperback Edition
Copyright © 2025 (As Revised) Brian Drake

Rough Edges Press
An Imprint of Wolfpack Publishing
1707 E. Diana Street
Tampa, FL 33610

roughedgespress.com

This book is a work of fiction. References to historical events, real people, or real places are used fictitiously. Any similarity to real persons, living or dead, is purely coincidental and not intended by the author.

All brand names and product names used in this book are trademarks, registered trademarks, or trade names of their respective holders. Wolfpack Publishing is not associated with any product or vendor in this book.

Paperback ISBN 978-1-68549-651-7
Ebook ISBN 978-1-68549-553-4

For Harlan

VENGEANCE STRIKE

SAM RAVEN STARED AT AN ELEPHANT.

It was a fascinating piece, gray and white, six stories all. Tourists took pictures in front of the massive form. Lucy the Elephant was a main attraction in Atlantic City. Reportedly the oldest roadside attraction in the United States, which Raven found fascinating; it also qualified as the ugliest. The most unusual. The most...*what the heck is it doing there?* kind of thing. He examined the stationary elephant and its impressive presentation. Sectional lines showed how each piece connected to make the elephant whole. But why would anybody want a picture next to the monstrosity? It seemed silly. Then again, he was in Atlantic City.

And he wasn't in town for fun. He was early to a meeting set to take place across the street. He'd scouted the neighborhood and the surrounding buildings for threads and found none. He hated to assume the worst, but he'd learned the hard way to do so no matter where he set foot in the world. With the recon out of the way, he wandered across the street to see the giant elephant.

The elephant's eyes were the worst feature. White circles against black; a caricature. The tusks and snout didn't look natural. Lucy wouldn't have qualified for cartoon status, but had somehow become a roadside attraction. But what the heck, it made people stop and take pictures and then wander to shops and restaurants. Raven bet the proprietors weren't complaining. Let the ugly thing sit and bring in the money. It was better than a poke in the eye with a sharp stick. And it couldn't have been as tacky as the rest of the nearby boardwalk, or the hotels and casinos trying to outdo Vegas with their gaudy lights and neon.

Raven fit in well with the tourists in his street clothes and tennis shoes. A blue jacket blocked the wind from the ocean, but there was no avoiding the salt-tinge in the air.

He watched two kids, boy and girl, break out in laughter. They were trying to climb one of the elephant's legs as their father snapped a picture. Raven felt for the locket hanging under his shirt. The little girl reminded him of another who'd have liked Lucy the Elephant, too. And Raven wished he was the father taking the picture. If his life had taken a different turn than it had, he would have been.

He shook away the thought and checked his watch. Meeting time. He turned from the ugly elephant and crossed the street at a crosswalk.

He'd welcomed the peaceful moment before the war without end began again, but the time had passed. Duty called.

IT WASN'T the fanciest meeting he'd ever attended.

The sign outside read "For Lease" and the building needed paint. Maybe other touch-ups considering the poor state of some of the wood. The corners of the roof, with their visible dry rot, needed the most attention. The barrage of ocean salt spray carried with the wind hadn't done any of the structures around him favors. Two cars sat parked outside; Raven's wasn't one of them. His rental was half a block away.

He went to the door and knocked twice.

A bearded man in a black suit answered. Built like a brick wall. Thick in the chest, arms, neck. His tailored blazer hid a pistol under his arm, but not so perfectly Raven missed the bulge.

The man said, "Yes?"

"I'm Sam Raven."

The man's grim features brightened. "Oh, of course." He opened the door and Raven stepped through. The big man shut the door. "Follow me. Mr. Ward is expecting you."

Raven held open his jacket to show the Nighthawk Custom Talon .45 autoloader in the shoulder speed rig. The big man waved him off.

Raven let the jacket cover the gun again.

They walked through an empty front room to a doorway. The big man stopped in the middle of the doorway and said, "He's here, sir." Then he stepped aside and gestured for Raven to enter.

Raven did so slowly. He kept the big man in his peripheral vision, in case of trouble. He didn't see any others in the room—why two cars?

There had to be more security men. But they were hiding.

Kendrick Ward sat behind a folding table with a laptop computer and file folders in front of him. He wore a suit like the big man, but gray; he looked a little older than Raven judging by the lines on his face. He was not bulky like his bodyguard. He had the soft features of a man accustomed to a sedentary lifestyle.

He stood as Raven approached and stuck out a hand.

"Mr. Raven. I'm Kendrick Ward. A pleasure."

They shook. His grip as strong. He spoke with force; he had no indoor voice.

"Thank you for coming to see me."

"No problem."

"Please, have a seat."

Raven frowned at the chair beside him. A metal folding job with dents. He only decided it was okay when he noticed Ward had a similar chair.

"Everything looks temporary," Raven said. He sat and crossed his legs.

"I own the building. It's been unoccupied for three months. I figured it was safest to meet you here."

"Is somebody threatening you?"

"Precautions," Ward said. "Did our go-between tell you much?"

"He said you might have a job for me, if I had an interest."

"And?"

Raven shrugged. "Nothing else."

It wasn't true. Raven had checked Ward out. He was a businessman in Atlantic City, real-estate and investment-related. Large fortune. Big house. Big family. But tragedy had struck the Wards same as it had Raven. He knew what the man wanted to talk about; he wasn't sure of the details. If the details proved satisfactory, Raven had every intention of taking the man's job.

To murder a man.

Raven said, "Is it only you and your assistant here?"

He tried not to laugh at calling the big bearded man an assistant. He sensed the fellow behind him, off to the left.

"Why do you ask?"

"There are two cars outside."

Ward smiled without humor. "I have other men here, in other rooms. Just in case."

"It's time to tell me what this is about," Raven said.

Ward tapped jittery fingers on one of the file folders. He opened the flap, turned it around, and pushed the folder towards Raven.

2

RAVEN PULLED THE FOLDER CLOSER AND EXAMINED THE contents. Glossy color photographs of a young woman. She wasn't very old, 18 at the most; the photo set contained annual school photos and a few candid shots at home. She appeared bright and happy with long blonde hair and dark eyes—the same dark eyes as the man sitting before him. Raven looked at the first two shots, but then skimmed the rest. He placed them back in the folder.

"One of your daughters, Mr. Ward?"

"My oldest. Francesca. We called her Francie."

Raven nodded. *Past tense.*

"The summer after she graduated high school, she, well, tried some things. Drugs, alcohol. You know what teenagers do. Somebody gave her heroin and she got hooked. She died from an overdose before the summer ended. Before my wife and I were to drive her to college."

"I understand," Raven said. "My condolences."

Ward took back the folder with his daughter's pictures inside. He moved hastily, like he wanted to snatch them from flame. The lines on his face seemed deeper now. He moved the folder to his left. The next folder he passed to Raven as well.

"I did some research," Ward said. "I called in a few favors, too. I wanted to know who sold the heroin, how it got into the country, and who brought the stuff into the city. I found my answers, and this is what the job is about." Ward opened the other file and Raven reached for it.

More pictures, but not of a young woman. The photos featured an olive-skinned male with thick black hair and a sturdy build. He liked expensive jewelry and clothes and wore both in every shot. He was quite striking; his image leaped off the page. Whoever he was, he was a man who gave orders. And his people followed those orders without fail. The pictures showed others around him who looked eager to receive those orders.

"I don't recognize this man," Raven said.

"You're looking at Martin Sevilla. He's a cartel boss in Colombia."

"His group brought in the heroin?"

"He supplies the distributors in this part of the state, yes. The pushers work for his representatives all over Atlantic City. Heroin, meth, etc. The usual menu. I know I don't have to spell it out to a man of your expertise, Mr. Raven."

Raven nodded. He was a man made for war. Once he'd worn the uniform of the 82nd Airborne and 5th Special Forces Group. Later he'd traded his officer patch for the anonymity of the CIA's Ground Branch. Now he was freelance. No uniform. No home. But still a warrior.

It wasn't the life he'd wanted. Raven had seen the worst the world had to offer and escaped for a quiet civilian life. Then fate dealt a cruel blow with sudden tragedy, and vengeance became his new mission. The only link to his past was the sterling silver locket around his neck. He never talked about what was inside, but it motivated his crusade.

He pursued the world's predators, those who created victims and heartache, to deliver justice one bullet at a time.

There were too many like Kendrick Ward in the world, too many who had suffered at the hands of evil men. He might not have been able to save the man's daughter, but killing the man responsible might bring the family desperately needed peace.

Raven paused on a photo of Sevilla inspecting a line of "troops." Raven didn't consider them real soldiers, though he wouldn't want to underestimate them in battle. The line of gunmen wore street clothes and held automatic rifles. A regular army in such a pose would look impressive, with sharp uniforms and faces etched with cold discipline. The men in the picture were nothing of the sort. They wore rough faces, had crazy eyes; they were the cannon fodder thrown to the front line. But they were still deadly.

Sevilla beamed at the line of gunners. Another man stood next to him, the instructor of the group. The instructor was shorter than Sevilla. "Do you know who this man is?" Raven said, showing the picture and tapping on the second figure.

"No. I only know Sevilla."

Raven flipped through more. "There are quite a few people in his entourage, aren't there?"

"If you see fit to identify them all, I won't stop you," Ward said.

Raven stacked the pictures on the table. "Tell me what you want."

"Can you not tell?"

"I need to hear it from you."

"I want Sevilla dead," Ward insisted, "and his drug-making operation destroyed."

Raven took a deep breath and let it out slowly. He and Ward didn't break eye contact. There were a few responses Raven could provide, but none Ward wanted to hear.

"Somebody will replace Sevilla very quickly," Raven said. "Another cartel will fill the gap. This always happens, every time one of these guys gets whacked. It's never long before the problem resumes."

"You're saying he's not worth killing?"

"I'm saying it's not going to change anything."

"The man who poisoned my daughter will be dead," Ward pointed out.

"And the next cartel will poison more daughters and sons. You'll keep me around full-time to deal with them."

"I have no intention of *that*, Mr. Raven."

"You need to understand the reality."

"I understand. Believe me, I do. We aren't going to wave a magic wand and end the drug problem. But I can ask you to end the life of the man who killed my daughter."

"The best course of action," Raven said, "is to not only take out Sevilla, but his immediate successors as well."

"Which does what?"

"Creates in-fighting among the survivors. All the fellows who think they deserve the captain's chair will kill each other off until only one remains. It interrupts the cycle for a short time. Kills off more of these snakes, too. It's a theory anyway."

"Is it truly a theory, or have you seen it first-hand?"

"Yes, and yes."

"Am I asking too much, Mr. Raven? Or will you take the job?"

"It will be expensive. I'll need time to hire the right people, organize some training and reconnaissance—"

"I have already hired five good men," Ward said. "They're stationed on property I own in Virginia." He woke the laptop from sleep mode and the displayed showed a map. Somewhere deep in a forest, a wide clearing surrounded by trees. *Very* isolated.

"Wait," Raven said. "You have a team. Why me?"

"I need you to lead the team."

"I'm not sure they'll appreciate me being there."

"They understood their role when I hired them. I explained I'd be calling in an expert to get them in shape and prepared. Somebody to act as the commanding officer. They were okay as long as I handed over a pile of cash. They're Americans, they have decent military records, and they hate the cartels as much as I do. One or two hate drugs for their own reasons."

"Uh-huh."

"You're not convinced."

Raven leaned back and folded his arms. "What else do you have?"

Ward began cycling through pictures on the computer. He stopped on a shot of a C-130 Hercules. "I have pilots ready to fly you to Colombia. A chopper crew to get you out. No expense spared." More pictures. Shots of a mansion— Sevilla's ornate home. A map of the property. Close shots of guards on duty.

"Where did you get these?"

"Well, um—"

"You have somebody on the inside?"

Ward laughed. "No, nothing of the sort. I told you, research and favors."

"Favors from whom?"

"People in—" Ward swallowed. "People in the service. In the government. People who *understand*, Mr. Raven."

"You mean a bunch of people who now *know* what you're doing once they put two and two together."

Ward tried to supply an answer but only stuttered.

3

WARD FINALLY PUSHED THE WORDS OUT.

"If it's the legality you're worried about—"

"What the FBI or anybody else in US law enforcement think doesn't concern me," Raven said. "If people know, they're going to talk. And if they talk, Sevilla's cartel is going to hear. And if Sevilla learns about this, he'll not only *vanish*, he will send somebody to shut you up. Permanently."

Ward swallowed.

"Are you prepared for such emergencies?" Raven said.

"It's why I have men with me. At my home—"

"Same crew?"

"Yes. I'm only—"

"Pissed off and looking for revenge. I understand."

"Do you?"

"I was in the same spot myself once. Until somebody told me to step back, calm down, and deal with the problem rationally. Or as rationally as one can in this situation."

"Are you suggesting I not do this?"

Raven considered his answer, and weighed a few possibilities in his mind.

"Increase your security at home. How many are we talking about right now? Today."

"I have four men who rotate day and night," Ward said.

"You want ten minimum. Find out who your current guys know, who they trust, and bring them aboard."

"Are you taking the job?"

"First, I want to meet your mercenaries, and see this property of yours, and look at all the data you have on Sevilla," Raven said.

"I'm paying the team a million dollars each. You get two million."

"We'll see," Raven said. "If the crew meets my standards, I'll take the job. I'd rather work with my own people, but they'll cost more."

"You'll find the men I selected more than satisfactory, Mr. Raven. I haven't succeeded as a businessman in this state by being a poor judge of character."

The meeting ended. Raven and Ward shook hands again, and the bearded man showed Raven out.

He returned to Caesars Atlantic City. His room overlooked the boardwalk and the ocean. Raven wasn't staying long, but decided the premium charged for the view was worthwhile. He liked watching the ocean at every opportunity. The cycle of the waves always offered a sense of peace. While he didn't have the soundtrack from the distance, he could still sit and watch.

He sat by the window enjoying the view while dialing a number on his cell. The number connected to a man overseas who answered on the third ring.

"How'd the meeting go?" asked a man named Oscar Morey.

Morey was a man who hadn't always been on the side of the angels. He'd been a big man in the European underworld once, but one who managed never to spend a day in jail. With ears to the ground in many areas, and contacts all over the world, there wasn't anything he didn't know, or could learn, if given enough time.

Years earlier, when a much younger Raven was in Paris to kill a man responsible for several murders, Morey intercepted him with a warning. *Stay out of our business. You don't want this kind of trouble.* Raven explained why his target had to die, and drew Morey to his side. Some crimes were too heinous for even Morey to tolerate, and he allowed Raven to finish his mission.

After Raven saved one of Morey's kids from certain death, the underworld legend pledged his support. From there, the bond between them grew stronger. Raven was smart enough to know when fortune handed him a talisman. In this case, a crusty old bastard named Oscar Morey. He was now retired from his old life, but acted as a go-between for Raven and potential clients. Ward had contacted Morey first, who then called Raven with the proposal.

"Ward is an interesting chap," Raven said. He sipped an ice-cold gin-and-tonic he'd mixed with his own supply.

After explaining the details, Oscar only replied with, "Hmmm."

"Not what you expected?"

"I think you're right to be concerned about word getting back to the cartel," Oscar said. "He's sloppy."

"It would have been better if he'd asked me to dig up all the data."

"He wanted to impress you."

"I am. Whoever took those photos was very close to the subject. Not a blurred imagine in the batch."

"What's your decision?"

"I told him I'd make up my mind after I met his team and

looked at the practice ground. If the guys are okay, I'll do it. Does his background check out?"

"He isn't lying," Oscar said. "At least he isn't lying about the daughter. It made the news."

"What about the fancy contacts he claims to have? What did he do in a past life to gain those people?"

"It's a mystery," Oscar said. "He never served a day in the military, and doesn't do any work with the government. Nothing I found suggests he even knows one end of a rifle from the other. Your guess is as good as mine, unless you ask him."

"Maybe I will."

"But he could be like us, Sam," Oscar said. "There could be details in his past that never made the official record."

"Fair enough."

"You're making the right call. Look at his setup, then decide."

"Right."

"Anything else?"

"Not for now. Thanks for taking the time to talk."

"I can't sleep anyway," Oscar said. "Been having a lot of nightmares lately."

"Guilty conscience?"

"If you only knew. See you."

Raven said good-bye and ended the call. He sat with his feet on the edge of the window still and watched the sun go down. Lights on the boardwalk soon brightened, blocking out the ocean view. He continued to watch where the ocean had been, and realized he was looking into pitch black. A void. The abyss. He waited for the abyss to look back.

He sympathized with Kendrick Ward. He was a father on a mission, a mission not unlike Raven's. They tragically complemented one another.

Tragedy united many who never knew the size of the club they belonged to.

An exclusive club.

The only standard of entry was to lose a part of yourself you could never get back.

4

"Look alive, bug-fucks!"

A tall man with close-cropped dark hair shouted the words. He was speaking to four other men who stopped what they were doing to line up. The wind generated from the whipping rotor blades of a chopper pushed at them. Trees surrounding the compound whipped to and fro. Raven surveyed the five men from the passenger seat. He turned back to shout a thank you to the pilot, then ducked his head as he climbed out. He didn't know why he always had the instinct to duck when around a helicopter. The blades were high enough. There was no chance of him having his head lopped off. But there was an instinct, an automatic reflex, that made him duck. He went with it. Because, heck, someday the blades *might* be low enough to give him a haircut, or worse.

The base camp wasn't terrible on the surface. It was settled in the V of two hills somewhere deep in Virginia's Blue Ridge Mountains. Open field for shooting, plenty of uneven terrain for running. Several buildings, nothing fancy, and access to a paved road about a mile away. Raven had spotted the road from the chopper before landing. The forest looked thick enough to conceal a party of mercenaries who'd be shooting a lot.

Raven turned his attention to the men. They waited fifteen yards away. He walked toward them as the chopper began to lift off. As it gained altitude, the noise faded; soon, only the wind made any noise. And Raven's boots. They crunched on the dried leaves peppering the ground.

Raven addressed the tall man. He stuck a hand out. "Sam Raven."

"I'm Ellison," the man said. "Kayson Ellison." The tall man pointed a big finger at each of the other mercs as he introduced them. "Here you got Archie; then Starkey, but we call him Fireplug; Chen; Marshall and Pope. We've been acting more like a construction crew than soldiers, sir."

"Why?"

"All these buildings needed work."

Raven nodded. "Call me Raven."

"We gonna actually blow something up real good or what?" Ellison said.

"I'm sure we will."

Raven introduced himself to each man. He wanted to know why they called Harry Starkey "Fireplug". When face-to-face with the man, the reason was obvious. Harry Starkey was the shortest of the group, but thick with muscle and solidly built. Just because he didn't clear five-foot-five didn't mean he had no ability to fight. At least Ellison and the rest hadn't gone for a dumb nickname like "Short Round" or "Short Stop."

The merc next to Starkey, Archie Marshall, introduced himself as the explosive expert. "If it goes boom, hand it to me," he said.

Next man in line, Caleb Chen, wore a tight tank top

exposing his arms and shoulders and the 101st Airborne tattoo on his right shoulder.

"I was in the 82nd," Raven said.

"Sorry to hear that," Chen said. "We can't all be the best."

Raven laughed.

David Pope had a cigar sticking out of his shirt pocket. Raven said, "I like Padrons."

"Really?" Pope removed the cigar. "This one's a Man O' War. Name fits, right?"

"Got any more?"

"I brought a box, yeah."

"I'll try one later, if it's all right."

"Sure."

With the exception of Fireplug Starkey and Kayson Ellison, the other three mercs ran to type. Tall, wiry, muscled; visible scar tissue; short haircuts. Perpetual soldiers.

"So, what's the score here?" Raven said. He turned back to Ellison.

"We built that," Ellison said. He pointed another big finger at the largest of the three structures in the compound. Two stories, with a balcony. "Best we can do for a mock-up of the Sevilla mansion," the tall man continued. "I'm not even sure it's going to do us any good. But it kept us busy while we waited on you, Raven. Basic kill house inside, even though we have no idea what the real interior layout looks like."

"Well, it's nice anyway," Raven said.

"Sure," Starkey said. "If the war doesn't work out, we can build condos."

Raven smiled. The wind ruffled his hair. He wasn't sure what to do with the crew, though they seemed all right.

"Listen up, guys," he said. The men crowded closer. "I didn't promise to take this job. I wanted to meet you first, and you all seem okay. What I want to see next is what you're working with to plan this attack."

Ellison jerked a thumb over his shoulder. "Back at the Taj Mahal, dude."

Raven looked over Ellison's shoulder. The "Taj Mahal" was a square building with white walls and a flat roof.

"You want a top bunk or a bottom bunk?" Ellison continued.

"Tell me there are showers," Raven said.

"Oh, we got showers, yeah," Ellison said.

"What's the catch?"

"No catch. Hot water and everything."

"Show me," Raven said.

Ellison started for the barracks. Raven followed. The other three men followed Raven.

The barracks looked clean on Raven's first scan. Bunks lined one wall. The beds were made and the floor around them tidy. A disciplined fighting crew was important. If the place had looked like a frat house, it wouldn't have mattered how well they assembled a building or fired a weapon. A lot of mercenaries threw discipline out the window; they were paid to fight, not sweep a floor. A crew who stuck to the basics was worth checking out further.

"We put our briefing area over here," Ellison said. He led Raven to the far end of the room. Tacked to the wall were several maps; one was the map Ward had shown Raven on the laptop. Some bore red circles in certain areas. Pinned pictures showed portions of Sevilla's mansion, but never the entire thing. From the map showing only the estate property, it looked like the house covered six acres alone. The rest of his compound, made up of other buildings, horse stables, garages, whatever else the *fashionable* cartel leader needed for living, covered more acreage.

The photos showed armed men wandering around, stationed at or near the house. Not all of them were shots he'd already seen. A cluster of Jeeps, some with mountain machine guns, some not, sat on the east side of the property. In some ways the material was hardly usable; the pictures didn't show enough to give them an idea of weak spots, or points of entry. In other ways, it was impressive for somebody like Ward to have collected.

"This is what you have to work with?" Raven said.

"For now," Ellison said. "The big guy is bringing us some video of the place."

"Big guy? Ward?"

"No, his bodyguard."

Raven nodded. The man who'd refused to hold onto Raven's gun when he went to sit down with Ward. *Talk about trust...*

Raven folded his arms. "We got any tea or something to drink?"

Ellison showed Raven to the tea kettle and propane-powered stove.

5

A LINE OF TARGETS SUPPORTED ON WOOD STAKES TOPPLED AS string after string of 5.56mm slugs ripped into them.

Raven watched with approval. The crew knew how to shoot, for sure.

Ward had provided a crate of Heckler & Koch HK416 rifles. Not a terrible weapon by any means, in fact the latest A5 version of the rifle, and a testament to Ward's buying power. Other weapons included SIG-Sauer 9 mm handguns, a variety of grenades, body armor, the works. None of the gear looked sub-standard. Used and beat up, yes. But cosmetic condition didn't matter as long as internals worked to spec. The HK rifles the crew fired, so far, worked up to spec and beyond.

Ellison wanted to see what the "new guy" could do. Was he a shooter or not? He and the crew reset the targets, offered Raven his choice of rifle, and told him to go to work.

Raven slapped a fresh 30-round mag into the weapon. He had to extend the stock to accommodate his length of pull. Fireplug laughed; it had been his weapon. Raven set the targets at 25-yeards; not hard shooting at all. He knew he wanted the job now; the crew had convinced him; but there were still a few kinks to work out. Specifically, in the planning of the actual mission.

The HK had a 10-inch barrel. Raven would have preferred a longer barrel, but for close-quarters, shorter was better. And the gun packed plenty of punch with the 5.56mm NATO projectiles double-stacked in the magazine.

He tucked the stock into his shoulder and worked the trigger.

There wasn't much space left on the oval targets, but Raven picked out a few white spots here and there. He put holes where he wanted, the rifle bucking comfortably against his shoulder. When he emptied the first mag, he slammed home another, and flicked the full-auto selector. His controlled 3-round bursts splintered the wooden stakes. The targets fell over one after another, each burst landing where intended. When he handed the now-empty but still-smoking weapon back to Fireplug, the stocky merc looked happy.

"You've done this a few times," he said.

"More than a few."

The day had begun with an early wake up and run through the forest, Raven in the lead. He took the men uphill, downhill, around and around. He stayed in the lead the length of the run, and nobody dropped out. Everybody showered and changed clothes after. Caleb Chen then fired up the propane grill and prepared breakfast. Raven tried to quiz him about who he knew in the 101st Airborne, wondering if they'd ever crossed paths. But Chen refused to acknowledge the 82nd Airborne existed. Raven took the ribbing with a laugh.

Shooting practice commended after breakfast.

"Pistols next," Raven announced.

They practiced with the SIG-Sauer P-226 handguns for a while. Raven offered the use of his Nighthawk Custom to anybody who wanted to try; nobody did. The young mercs dismissed the 1911-style Nighthawk as a "geezer gun". The gun Raven had carried for many years. The gun that had saved his life countless time. This time, Raven only shook his head. A generation who'd grown up on "plastic Glocks" had no affection for all-steel works of art. It surprised him they even bothered with the SIGs. Then again, the SIGs were nine-millimeter, and held a lot of bullets—more bullets is more better! Raven's .45 only held a paltry eight rounds.

After lunch, as they sat around a picnic table, Ellison asked the question on everybody's mind.

"You leading this charge or what, Raven?"

"I'll do it. I can't have some other—what do you call them?"

"*Bug* fucks," Ellison said.

"Right. Can't have some other bug fuck leading you into battle. It's gotta be done by somebody not here for the money."

"We all here for the money," Ellison said. "Nobody tryin' to be a hero."

"What he's saying, cock breath," Starkey said to Ellison, "is that he actually likes us. Unlike *some* people I can think of."

"I don't dislike anybody," Ellison said, "I just can't stand *you* fuckers."

Raven let the men rib each other while he slipped away to call Ward. He confirmed the job and told the business man to get back in touch with Oscar Morey. Morey would provide instruction on how to transfer the two million.

But Raven had other questions.

"I hear your man is coming with some video footage."

"Yes," Ward said. "Did you meet him when we talked?"

"I didn't get his name."

"Fox," Ward said. "Zac Fox. Been with me for years. He'll

be there tomorrow, by helicopter, with more on Sevilla's place."

"Okay."

"How are things going?"

"Good crew, but the pictures and maps you provided aren't enough to give us a real idea of what we're facing. What are we going to see in this video?"

"I'm not sure."

"I need to see inside the mansion."

"And I hope my cameraman was able to get inside," Ward said. "I haven't seen it."

"You're pretty good for a humble businessman."

"Friends in low places," Ward said, laughing, before saying good bye.

Raven interrupted his farewell. "You increase your security?"

"Working on his as we speak, Mr. Raven."

"Okay."

Raven let the other man hang up first. He returned to the mercs, who were still laughing and giving each other a hard time. Raven yelled for them to quiet down.

"I'm official," he said, "and Zac Fox will be here tomorrow to bring us some video of the target."

Fireplug Starkey frowned. "Did you say *Zac* Fox?"

"Yeah. Why?"

"Son of a bitch..."

"Want to share with the rest of us?"

"I knew a Zac Fox back in Queens," the short man said. "Loan shark. My father used him once. When Dad couldn't pay, Fox broke one of his arms. I swore if I ever caught up with him, I'd return the beating with interest."

David Pope sounded off. "Don't go blowing my million bucks, shorty."

"You don't even know if it's the same guy," echoed Caleb Chen.

"How many guys are named Zac Fox?" Starkey said.

"I'll Google it," said Ellison.

Archie Marshall, the explosive expert, said nothing. Raven noticed he hadn't heard Marshall join in the teasing.

"Everybody calm down," Raven said. "Starkey, let's assume it's a different guy for now. He's going to bring our stuff, and we're going to continue practice. Okay?"

Starkey let out a huff.

"I said, okay, Starkey?"

"Fine," Fireplug said.

"Let's clean this up and get back to shooting," Raven said. "In fact, we're going to try the little kill house you built. Try not to knock it down, okay?"

6

RAVEN DIDN'T WANT ANY TROUBLE WHEN ZAC FOX showed up.

He stood alone as the helicopter carrying Ward's representative descended. Emailing the video to the training compound might have been easier, but Ward had elected not to do so. He wanted the DVD handed from one person to another for security reasons. He didn't ask Ward what he'd do if they lost the video because the helicopter crashed.

The chopper didn't crash. It landed softly in the open area and Raven walked toward the flying machine, ducking his head as usual. The rotor wash created a small dust storm, kicking up small pieces of debris to fling them far and wide. The side door opened, and Zac Fox gestured for him to hurry. The big bearded man didn't wear a suit this time. He was in casual clothes with a blazer and no handgun under his coat. This time. He remained strapped to his seat.

He held out a sealed manila envelope; Raven took it.

"Call the boss if you have questions!" Fox shouted over the turning blades. Raven gave him a thumbs up and started back. The chopper rose and tipped forward to fly over the treetops. And away.

Raven slit the seal as he walked back to the main building. Or what he called the "main" building; *bunk house* was a better term. He pulled open the door to go inside. Fireplug met him.

"I swear it's him," the short man said.

"You're sure?"

"I watched through binoculars, Raven. He's older and didn't have the beard but he's got the look in his eyes I remember."

"All right." Raven went inside. Fireplug followed.

"What are you going to do?"

"Me? The man attacked *your* family, Starkey. You want out of the mission?"

"No! I need the money. But you gotta say something. At least ask Ward if he knows."

"How come you're only saying something now? Did you not meet Fox when Ward hired you?"

"Ward wasn't alone when he hired me but he didn't have *that* asshole with him."

Raven nodded. There were always problems in any outfit. Somebody always got jumpy. But Fireplug's accusations made him wonder something else. Did Ward have an employee affiliated with organized crime? Even a two-bit loan shark operation? What other connections did he have? And did those connections provide the intelligence material tacked to the walls?

"I'll talk to Ward."

"That's all?"

"What else can I do, Starkey?"

Fireplug scoffed but didn't argue further. He joined the others. The mercenaries sat around a wide-screen television while Raven inserted the DVD. He felt their eyes on him.

One of their own had asked a reasonable question, and he'd yet to answer. He truly wanted to talk to Oscar Morey first, see what his friend could dig up, maybe find information he missed on his first pass. But he had to admit it appeared he was dodging Fireplug's concern. He wasn't. But he couldn't call a halt to the mission to deal with Fireplug's assertions. They only had a week left to make a plan.

When he called, he had to do so in front of the crew. They had to see him take charge of the problem, otherwise he'd lose their confidence.

The DVD had no label or any markings to indicate what was on the disk. Raven pressed the DVD player tray closed.

"Let's see what we got," Raven said. He pressed Play and moved back.

KAYSON ELLISON WANTED to give Raven the benefit of the doubt.

But a lifetime of looking over his shoulder, not trusting anybody, clouded his judgement.

He sat at the end of a ratty couch with legs crossed and arms folded, skeptical of what appeared on screen. He believed Fireplug Starkey; the man was far too adamant about Fox to have been lying.

Which made him wonder about Ward.

Which made him wonder about Raven.

Ellison grew up in Chicago, where his father and grand-father ran a trucking company. He'd seen his share of mobbed up characters come through looking for protection money. Often, they tried to arrange no-show jobs for convicts on parole. His pop and grandpop did what they had to do to make sure the doors stayed open and business ran smoothly. Now and then, keeping the doors open meant doing business with bad people. And Ellison never forgot the men with the smirks and haughty eyes. They were men who believed they could get away with anything, including murder.

Instead of joining his family in the business, he enlisted in the Army. It was the only way out of the gangs and the poverty he grew up around. He didn't want the stink of his upbringing to carry through to adulthood. But it was too late. Ellison had trust problems. He had problems with authority. He did contract work because at least he could pick the jobs and decide who he wanted to answer to. And while Raven had seemed promising at the start, he wasn't so sure about the man now.

He kept quiet as the crew watched the footage on the television.

ARCHIE MARSHALL WATCHED the video with a careful eye. The explosives expert wanted to find places to plant bombs.

Marshall was a man of few words who always faded into the background no matter where he was. His leaning toward silence and anonymity wasn't because he was anti-social. In reality, he had little to say, and preferred to concentrate on his bombs rather than human interaction. An explosive demanded nothing but one's silent attention. He liked the intricate detail of proper wiring. He liked the effectiveness of a well-placed bomb. A blast at the right time saved lives and brought an end to a fight before too many of his friends fell to enemy bullets.

The video filled the screen.

Whoever took the footage carried the camera low, and filmed as they walked. The picture shook a little, and the camera lens never stayed on one part of the grounds for long. Sevilla's mansion was the first featured item. The sprawling home was too big to capture in the area the camera man stood. Marshall spotted the roof support columns right away. They also supported a front-facing balcony. Take those out, the top level would come crashing down.

"Does that balcony lead to the master bedroom?" Marshall asked.

David Pope was close to the wall map. He left his chair and leaned close to examine the map's notation. "Yes."

"Okay." Marshall said no more.

More footage showed the area beyond the mansion. Guards milled about; they all carried automatic rifles and looked eager to use them.

Then the camera settled on a woman.

7

CALEB CHEN LET OUT A LOW WHISTLE. "WHO IS SHE?"

Pope found a file on a table; he read fast. "Sevilla's daughter, Yasmina. She controls part of her father's distribution network." He set the file down.

Yasmina Sevilla was a striking figure; long black hair, toned physique. She wore loose camo shorts and tight green tank top. All she lacked to complete a military look were dog tags around her neck. She brought a Jeep to a stop as the camera lens found her. Nobody rode with her. Jumping out of the vehicle, she moved quickly toward the mansion. Somebody called out to her; she yelled back. She had no time to talk, she said. She had to see her father. The woman passed out of the frame, and the camera didn't stay with her.

"We didn't get to see the booty!" Chen called.

"Is she a target, too?" Ellison asked.

Raven shook his head.

"Great," Ellison said. "We'll whack the old man and she'll slide into his seat. Business as usual, uninterrupted, like we were never there."

Raven silently agreed. He used the remote to turn off the television. He said, "Is anybody as underwhelmed as I am?"

"It's a good effort," Pope offered. "But not anything we can use. It's nice to see some detail we don't have in the pictures or on the map, though."

Raven walked to the map on the wall. He examined the pictures, the circles on the map. "A frontal assault is off the table," he said. "Agreed?"

"Totally," Pope said. "With so few of us, and a place as big as Sevilla has, his men will wipe us out before we get to him. The guards know all the nooks and crannies."

"We'll find a few of our own," Chen said.

"This has to be smart," Raven said. His back was still to the team as he looked at the wall. "What are Sevilla's habits? Where does he go? He can't stay at home all the time."

"Best to find out when we get there," said Ellison. "Watch the place a while. It's not like we have a hard deadline."

"But we can't take too long, either," Raven said. "I don't like how many people Ward has spoken to about this."

"You don't trust him either?" Ellison said.

"All I can say is I have questions of my own. But I'm too big a do-gooder to let them get in the way right now."

"Nobody likes these drug pushers," Pope said, "but what if Ward is holding back?"

"What might he be holding back?"

"I don't know. Just guessing."

"No, you're not," Raven told him. He turned to face the man. Pope averted his gaze. "You think this is a set-up."

Pope shook his head.

"But for whom?" Chen asked. "Ward doesn't have a beef with us, he's paying a ton of money, probably more than a job like this deserves. But what if—"

"Based on what evidence?" Raven said to Pope. "That Fox fellow?"

"Well—"

Raven scanned the faces of the other men. They expected him to supply the answer. Instead, he took out his cell phone from a back pocket.

"All right, let's call Ward right now and ask him what's up."

Raven dialed. He clicked the button to put the call on speaker. He wanted them all to hear the conversation.

"Yes, Mr. Raven? Is there a problem?"

"Who is Zac Fox?" Raven said.

"Excuse me?"

"We have a concern we need to talk about, Mr. Ward," Raven said. "One of the guys says he knows Zac Fox from the old days. Says he used to work for a loan shark and injured one of his family members. He's a little upset at seeing him again. Care to elaborate?"

"Wait...what?"

"It's not a complicated question, Mr. Ward."

"It's not complicated, but I don't understand. Why is this a problem?"

"I'd like to avoid anybody getting hurt or killed who doesn't deserve it. I'd like to get into Colombia with all the men you hired, not four, because one decided to scoot."

"Do we have to talk about this now? I have—"

"Cancel or have somebody tell them you'll be late. Because, yes, we're talking about this right now."

"Hang on."

The line went silent a moment. Raven kept his eyes off the men. But they watched him.

"I'm back," Ward announced. "Now, what do you want to know?"

"Was Zac Fox ever a loan shark, and did you know when you hired him? If not, please tell us how we're wrong."

"Zac Fox indeed has a past he'd rather not talk about,"

Ward said. "But we had to discuss it prior to my hiring him. He's done prison time for past crimes. He is certainly not going to go back to the kind of life he left behind. He's been open and honest with me about his background, I assure you. I hired him because I needed a security specialist. I also wanted somebody who knew some of the, um, *individuals* I'm forced to do business with from time to time."

Ellison stifled a curse and shook his head. Raven glanced at Starkey. The short man watched with rapt attention.

"Did I provide a satisfactory answer, Mr. Raven?"

Raven raised an eyebrow at Starkey.

Starkey nodded and mouthed "okay."

"Satisfactory, Mr. Ward."

"Good! I don't want anybody to doubt where I'm coming from with this. Was the video helpful?"

"It was fine," Raven said. "We're uncertain about how you're getting this information. It's not coming from government sources. Who do you know?"

"This is not the time to discuss those details," Ward said. "And I'd rather not put people at risk who are risking everything to help me. I'm late enough as it is. If there's nothing else—"

"Fine. For now."

"Yes. Quite." Ward hung up.

Raven put the phone away. He addressed the team. "Are we happy?"

Starkey answered, "I'm gonna bust that son of a bitch's head open when we get back."

"Emphasis," Raven said, "on *when we get back*. Okay?"

"I'm cool," Starkey said.

"Anybody else have a comment?"

"Yeah," Ellison said. "Can we stop talking *bullshit* and get on with business? You idiots need to quit being paranoid. Ward's got help. His help is *our* help, so shut up."

He grinned at Raven.

Raven sensed he'd overcome any last-second doubts Ellison may have had about him.

Fair enough.

Time to discuss the plan.

8

RAVEN FOLLOWED THE SCENT OF CIGAR SMOKE.

He found David Pope sitting in a lounge chair near an unused building. The stars were bright and covered the night sky. More stars than Raven often saw in any city. He often forgot how many you could see when removed from urban environments.

He noticed an extra chair beside Pope. "Is that for me?"

"Been waiting for you," Pope said. As Raven sat, Pope passed him a Man O' War cigar, cutter, and lighter. Raven snipped the end, toasted the tip, and took the first puffs.

"Not bad," Raven said. The flavor was rich and robust and packed a punch.

"I can never sleep before a job," Pope said. "Chopper's coming early, right?"

"Uh-huh." Raven puffed on the cigar.

"But when we get on the plan to Colombia, I'll pass right out. Every time. Never fails."

"Your subconscious tells you to finally relax," Raven said. "It's not uncommon."

"What about you?"

"I'll sleep like a log and be wide awake the whole flight."

"You think we got a chance?"

"We have a chance," Raven said. "The important thing is to pick the right time. We'll watch what Sevilla does and get him when he's not surrounded by a hundred guys."

"Me and Chen are going to quit when we're done with this job. Take our money and open a restaurant."

"I got the feeling he has the food business in his background," Raven said. Chen had done all the cooking during his stay, as well as before.

"His old man had a Chinese restaurant in California. Oakland, I believe. He taught Chen all he knows. Me? I'm the business manager. My old man ran a slew of companies and went bankrupt every time."

Raven frowned. "Did you learn anything useful?"

"I learned what not to do." Pope laughed. Raven smiled.

The money Ward had doled out was life-changing for some. For Raven? It would fill his account. Some who needed help could pay; some couldn't. He took as much as possible from those who could to be able to help those who didn't have access to the same resources. Ward's two million would go a long way.

"A good bourbon usually goes well with one of these," Raven said.

"I quit drinking five years ago."

"Good for you."

"For a while it looked like the booze would get me before the bad guys," Pope said. "I decided I was pushing my luck—after I got locked up for drunk driving during a blackout."

Raven didn't ask any questions. If Pope wanted to tell him more, he'd do so on his own. And he didn't. They sat and smoked and stared at the stars. The same stars they'd see in Colombia while searching for an opportunity to kill a Martin Sevilla.

THE SEVILLA ESTATE was twenty miles south of Bogota in a dense portion of the forest. Two-lane roads wound through the area. On the map, the road looked like the splayed tentacles of an octopus sleeping off a hangover. But only one road led to and from Sevilla's front gate.

Raven and the mercenaries parachuted from the back of Ward's C-130. As he said he would, Pope slept the entire flight. Raven had to shake him awake to get ready for the jump. When the back gate of the Hercules lowered, they stared out at blue sky and the dark green forest floor below.

They landed ten miles from the estate. The forest was warm and wet from high humidity. They began to sweat hard immediately. Five days of supplies—nobody wanted to have to visit Bogota for more. They didn't want to risk the natives noticing them. Everyone would talk about the strange Americans. The cartel had spies in every alley— they'd be ratted out before firing the first shot.

A short march to find camp. They took it slow, hiking up and down hill, watching for booby-traps and patrols. When they found a clearing near a stream, the team set up beside the water.

Raven spread out the map of Sevilla's property and began giving assignments. He wanted eyes on the mansion. He wanted the road investigated for ambush points.

He assigned Pope and Marshall to watch the mansion.

Ellison and Starkey took the road.

Raven and Chen had another task.

THE FARM WAS A GROW FIELD. Rows and rows of drug crops, tall green stalks almost neck high. It wasn't corn they were growing—the plants had too many leaves. Three aging barns storing the gathered crop dotted the ten acres. Smaller buildings at the south end processed the crops into cocaine and heroin.

It was the closest drug farm to Sevilla's estate; it was not his only one.

Raven and Chen made mental notes as they watched from a distance. Electrified fence around the perimeter. A staff of mostly farm hands. Six armed guards. But two of the guards patrolled with dogs—big Dobermans.

Still, it made for a soft target. An opening salvo to get Sevilla's attention.

The team returned to the camp after nightfall to compare notes.

Pope and Marshall reported Sevilla might be getting ready to drive somewhere.

Pope explained how one of Sevilla's men spent the day changing the oil on an armored Mercedes. He checked the tires, tested the alternator and battery, and washed the vehicle. Either it was a regular service, or Sevilla needed to drive long-distance.

Raven said he'd bet on a long drive.

Ellison and Starkey used the map to point out a good ambush point. The road had a tight turn two miles from the estate. The curve was sharp enough to force any driver to slow. Taking the curve too fast would send them off the road and down a slope, or into the rock face of a mountain.

Raven wanted everybody at the curve bright and early. He told Pope to return to the estate and radio them when the Mercedes departed. He needed Marshall at the road to place a few strategic bombs where they'd be most effective.

9

DAY TWO.

David Pope let the bugs crawl over him. He was one with the foliage around him. Not only did he wear full camouflage, complete with a floppy hat, but green and black paint streaked his face. The makeup only made his blue eyes more prominent. His pistol rode on his right hip, and he held the HK416 out in front. Aimed at the ground.

He lay on the tip of a hill, trees above, and kept his breathing slow. The heat and humidity squeezed him in a vice; Pope ignored the discomfort.

The Mercedes sat under a covered parking area, untouched. Nobody had gone near it in the three hours Pope had been at his vigil. He wondered if they were wrong. If Sevilla wasn't going anywhere after all. If the mechanic had only performed regular maintenance on the vehicle. Only more time would tell.

Activity around the mansion was minimal. Grounds keepers mowed grass, collected debris from around the house. A crew power-washed windows and the white stucco exterior.

Armed guards roamed lazily with slung weapons.

They weren't expecting trouble.

Pope's vantage point covered the eastern side. Sevilla liked to garden. In the back of the house, before the pool, a large plot housed roses and tomato plants.

His point of view also showed him a portion of the stone wall circling the estate. Steel spikes poked through the top edge, spikes with steel barbs on the sides. A wire ran along the length, connected to the tips of each spike. Pope didn't think the wire was electrified. Instead, he figured it was a sensor wire. A break in the chain would alert the gun crews to an intruder and tell them where to go to intercept.

Two figures approached the garden. They were talking, but Pope was too far away to hear. He pulled a pair of binoculars to his eyes. Sevilla and another man. They stopped to admire the growing tomatoes. Sevilla wore slippers and a thick bathrobe despite it being past noon. He didn't look like somebody preparing for a long car ride.

Wrong guess, Raven. Now what?

Pope watched the two men talk. The man with Sevilla used his hands for emphasis. Sevilla listened and replied with his hands in the pockets of the robe.

Pope hadn't seen the other man arrive, and saw no indication he'd shown up prior to beginning surveillance. The man was part of the house staff.

Pope wished he could hear what they spoke about.

MARTIN SEVILLA EARNED the right to relax now and then. He hadn't bothered changing out of his pajamas and wore the robe over them.

He was tall and well-built, dark hair and eyes; his attention shifted as the other man spoke. Sevilla had grown up always checking behind his back for the friend who wanted to betray him. With a knife blade between the ribs. He'd risen to power only because he'd killed them first. But old habits were hard to break. He still kept watch despite his position, money, power; none of it protected him. There was always somebody who wanted a piece.

Such was the topic of discussion as he and the other man admired the tomatoes.

His chief of intelligence, Nathan Meza, didn't take liberties with his attire. He wore casual white, shirt and trousers, with good running shoes and a pistol on his left hip.

And they weren't talking about tomatoes.

"They're moving ahead," Meza said, barely acknowledging the garden. "Chatter says they want to link up with mafia elements in New York City."

"I'll kill them all for this," Sevilla said in a low voice. He studied the ripening tomato vines. "The East Coast is *my* territory. He knows better than this."

"If we go on the offensive, I suggest you move out of the area. Maybe even go to your place in Honduras."

Sevilla wasn't only concerned with drug production and distribution. He owned interest in several Honduran tobacco farms, too. Cigarette and cigar production was a great way to launder money.

"I'm not sure we'll need to," Sevilla said. "A war isn't good for us. It will drain resources, and Panadero has plenty of his own to spare. But the DEA effort in Bogota is focused on *him.* They need evidence to make moves of their own. A few words in the right ear, a package of information, perhaps, will keep Panadero occupied. He'll forget trying to make new connections."

"It's worth a try," Meza agreed.

"He's hurting and everybody knows it," Sevilla said. "He's

made stupid decisions and it's cost him. The attempt at getting product into Italy was an utter failure."

"His shipments kept getting hijacked."

"Right. He's on the edge and a push off the cliff is all we need."

"I'll come up with some options," Meza said.

"Who's he working with in the US? Or did he send his own representatives?"

"He's not sent anybody," Meza said. "He has a connection with a businessman in New Jersey who gets around."

Sevilla nodded. "I see. Who is this man?"

"His name's Ward. He has two grown children in college and a wife who volunteers for various local organizations. Shall we—"

Sevilla waved off the unspoken suggestion. "I'm not messing around inside the US. We're not desperate enough yet. And we don't need to be if we play our cards right."

"Very good."

"Let me know what you find."

Meza nodded, turned, and walked away. Sevilla remained in the garden looking at his work. He didn't get to spend as much time with his hands in the dirt, but the results so far looked good. Roses bloomed brightly, red and yellow, the smell took him to a peaceful place. The tomatoes were ripening better than expected. He smiled. He might have to look over his shoulder till he died, but his work provided a level of comfort he appreciated, too.

POPE WATCHED the man to whom Sevilla spoke walked away, back into the house. Sevilla examined his garden.

He lowered the binoculars. Time to call Raven on the radio.

Pope plugged the wireless earpiece into his left ear.

"Pope to Raven."

It took a second for Raven to respond.

"Go."

"He's not going anywhere, chief. Still in his bathrobe and talking shop with somebody else in the garden."

"Copy. Stand by."

Pope waited. A rustle on his left—he looked. No threats. Only the movement of leaves as one bug or another went about its day. Another insect crawled across his neck. He made no move to swat. If he was going to be part of the environment, he had to *be* part of the environment.

10

LEMONADE OUT OF LEMONS AND ALL THAT. They hit the production farm first. Raven's idea: draw Sevilla out of his home to inspect the damage. Archie Marshall, the quiet bomb expert, started them off. *With a bang*, he joked to himself. Trying to defeat an electrified fence wasn't hard, but also wasn't easy, and took time. One could bypass the time and difficulty by blowing it up instead. Marshall endorsed the idea without argument.

He had two tasks. Blow the fence to let the others through, then make for the first row of stalks. He'd then set a phosphorous charge to set them ablaze. They weren't worried about an out-of-control fire. Every drug farm had its own fire suppression system. And they worked as long as somebody was alive to flip the switch.

Marshall, on his belly, crawled across the ground, dragging over the dirt. He tried to keep the noise to a minimum. But it was dark, the trees blocked the star and moonlight, and nobody could see with such low illumination anyway. His weight crunched, rustled, and snapped the thick foliage and ground growth. He paused every two inches—it seemed. He stopped a lot to not arouse attention from the guards. The rest of the team had their eyes on the security. They'd alert him through the wireless earbud in his right ear should a problem arise. Such as a sentry getting too close to him. As long as the wireless gear worked, of course. Marshall had seen too many fail, at least with bombs, where interference blocked remote detonation signals, to fully trust the gear.

Closer. *Snap.* Another twig went to its great reward.

Closer.

"Hold it, Archie."

Ellison's voice. Marshall froze in place. A fence post lay only a few feet ahead. He heard the electrified buzz of the wires.

"On your left. No dog."

The Dobermans would sniff him out fast and compromise the mission.

Marshall remained silent. *Small miracles.*

"I got him sighted," Ellison continued. "If he spots you, I'll take him out."

And alert the whole camp, Marshall thought. Bye-bye surprise. *Shit happens.*

Marshal smelled the guard's body odor before the armed man stepped into view. *Heat and humidity suck.* The gunner looked thin under a uniform too large for him; in the dark, Marshall couldn't see his face.

The guard spit at the fence. The saliva hit on a wire and sizzled. The gunner laughed to himself and continued out of sight.

"Stay put," Ellison advised. "He ain't far enough away yet."

Marshall remained still and silent for another few moments.

"All right, he's gone," Ellison reported.

Marshall crawled forward, finally reached the fence, and prepared his bomb. It wasn't fancy. A half-block of C4 with a timed detonator. He'd set the timer for thirty seconds before starting out.

"Am I clear?" he asked.

Ellison: "Clear my side."

Raven, watching from another position: "Nobody coming. Go for it, Archie."

Marshall stopped a foot form the fence and placed the C4 in the dirt. He activated the timer; the seconds ticked silently. Then he jumped to his feet and ran. Damn the noise—he needed cover *fast.*

He dived behind a big tree with a rippled layer of thick bark. Hands covering the back of his neck, he counted the last seconds in his head.

"Bombs away," he radioed.

The blast shook the ground. A ball of fire plumed.

RAVEN WATCHED from the southeast corner.

They'd observed the farm for over an hour, noting all farm hands gone for the night. Only the guards and dogs remained, and still a small force. Only six guys and two dogs.

Sweat trickled down the exposed portions of his skin; the night was warm, the humidity still thick. Bugs nipped at him. Luckily the farm didn't employ an outer patrol. They focused all security inside the electrified fence.

Marshall said, "Bombs away."

Raven averted his eyes from the explosion. He didn't want the momentary brightness to affect his night vision. The ground rumbled; the blast fed off the available oxygen and the flare lit the area before fading. Marshall would be the first man through, but Raven would have preferred he go first. He was team lead; it was his responsibility. But his position prevented him from doing so. As the farm guards reacted with yells and shouted, he bolted from cover. He ran hard, slicing through the thick leaves around him, stomping hard as he aimed for the smoking gap. The fire from the blast lit some foliage on fire, further aiding his navigation. Thick smoke hung in the still air.

Raven ran through, followed by Ellison. He caught sight of Marshall sprinting for the stalks. Between the fence and the stalks was a gap of about thirty feet. It was a short sprint, but also a wide-open shooting gallery. Raven went right, Ellison to the left. Their HKs crackled single shots as they engaged the on-coming sentries.

A heavy-machine gun started up, short bursts hammering through the chaos. Pope on the job, behind the team's US M-60. He covered the western side, from a rise, and had a good view of the battle ground.

Raven ran for a pair of wooden buildings ahead. Two sentries emerged from the shadows. One released a Doberman, who zeroed on Raven at speed like a heat seeking missile. Two shots—the dog flopped dead. *Sorry, pooch.* He raised his aim and fired again. The two sentries took cover between the buildings. Raven reached the first one, smashed a window, and tossed a phosphorous grenade. Any production equipment inside was about to go up in flames. He circled the back. One of the sentries tried to meet him halfway. Raven's HK kicked twice—man down. The second tried to come from behind. Raven pivoted to face him, but the guard charged, colliding like a runaway semi-truck, knocking Raven off his feet. He braced for the impact with the ground. The landing knocked the wind out of him, and the sentry rolled away to bring up his submachine gun.

Raven's rifle popped again, two small holes appearing in the sentry's chest. Raven fired a third and fourth time. The sentry fell to the side. Raven rose with a grunt, hearing Ellison's voice in his ear:

"East side, we need help!"

11

RAVEN TOSSED ANOTHER PHOSPHOROUS GRENADE THROUGH the window of the second building. Smoke already billowed from the first; orange flame flickered through the windows. Then he broke into a run for the east side of the farm.

"I'm behind you, Raven!" Marshall shouted.

Raven didn't look back. He saw the problem right away. More than one guard had taken cover in a barn; they were firing through openings. The cartel troops had Ellison and Starkey pinned down behind a stack of crates.

Raven ran toward them. Bullets smacked the ground at his feet. Marshall pitched a grenade. It landed short, the blast tearing a chunk out of the ground instead of the barn. But the explosion and eruption of dirt blocked the gunners from firing. Raven stopped beside Ellison; Starkey lay prone, trying to fire around the side.

Marshall ran behind them, circling around to one wall of the barn. Raven flipped his HK to full auto and peppered the barn with bursts. "Go!" he shouted to Ellison and Starkey. Both men bolted after Marshall.

Pope on his ear: "I can't cover you guys from where I'm at!"

"Water's warm!" Raven said. "Dive in."

Raven ran after his teammates as a salvo slammed into the pallets. The high-velocity slugs turned the solid pieces of wood into splinters. Soon Raven was out of view and heading for the barn. Marshall applied a charge to the wall and told them to get back. They did, getting flat; the blast knocked a gaping hole in the wall and Ellison threw a grenade. It exploded as two gunners tried to block the entry. The two men screamed as the concussion ripped their bodies apart.

DAVID POPE HAD ALWAYS LIKED the US M-60 machine gun. The belt-fed monstrosity was the perfect weapon, short of a nuke, to reach out and touch your enemies.

His short bursts covered the guys, but as he watched, he saw them doing well enough without him. When Raven disappeared around the back of the processing building, he'd held his breath a moment; then Raven reappeared. All well.

But the engagement at the barn was too far for him to provide any cover. The tall stalks were in the way.

And they were starting to burn. Marshall's phosphorus bomb touched off a small blaze; it grew by the minute. The flames crawled slowly, eating away at the poisonous plants. Heavy smoke drifting through the camp. The flames, visible against the night sky, had to show elsewhere, too. There was no wind; the smoke hung like a cloud. They needed him on the opposite side, and he'd rather not go charging through smoke to reach the barn. But he didn't see any other way.

Caleb Chen manned the M-60 with Pope. He helped feed the ammo belt; he'd be there to change the barrel if it got too hot, too. Both men rose. Pope clutched the machine gun while Chen held onto the ammo.

The M-60 was a great weapon, but not a great gun to move with urgency. The heavy weapon and ammo strained his arm muscles. No matter. Their friends needed help. He and Chen stopped long enough to squeeze over the fence wires like a boxer entering a ring. Then they charged headlong into the smoke. Pope had an idea where to set up. But he had to get there in time.

RAVEN ENTERED THE BARN FIRST. He cut to the left. Ellison and Starkey followed. They turned on the lights mounted to the Pic rails of their HK416s. Probing the darkness with the powerful lights, they searched for more targets. By Raven's count, there ought to have been two more sentries to deal with.

The fight had gone on too long already, but they couldn't pull back with an enemy at their heels.

The aging cocoa leaves hung on racks stacked to the ceiling. The formerly green leaves were turning brown. Soon they'd be ready for processing into cocaine and heroin.

"We're clear," Ellison said.

"Clear here," Raven said from his side. "Archie, light 'em up."

"Way ahead of you," Marshall said. He was already kneeling in front of one rack to set up another phosphorous charge. "Timer's set, let's go!"

They headed for the double-doors at the front. Smoke drifted in from the stalk fire. Raven took a quick look. No threats. Then he spotted movement, shadows along the ground that didn't belong.

He knew for sure when a salvo of rounds stitched the

wood over his head. He fired back, moving away from the door. The others got down as more slugs chewed the front wall. Smoke filled the barn as the phosphorous did its work.

"Gettin' warm in here, dawg!" Ellison shouted.

"Fall back to where we came in," Raven said. He fired one burst, then another, out the door, but had no targets to line up. For all he knew, the last two troops were already on the other side to make a flanking attempt.

Raven charged ahead of the others as they ran. He reached the hole in the wall first, then jumped back—yup, they were there. A bullet tugged at his uniform top as he rolled out of the way. He felt another smack the floor near his face.

"Stay down!" Pope shouted over the radio. The thumping M-60 joined the party.

POPE DIDN'T HAVE time to set his tripod mount. He kneeled as Chen held the ammo belt, and supported the M-60 with his free hand. The gun was too heavy to lift to his shoulder and aim. He fired from the hip, watching the impact of his rounds as they struck the ground, raising the muzzle. The two gunners converging on the barn spun around. One kept spinning as rounds cut through him, spurts of blood erupting from his back. Chen let out a "Hell, yeah!" The other sentry fired a burst and rolled. Pope tracked him, fired again, and missed. The gunner pitched a grenade—into the barn! Pope settled the muzzle in the gunner's direction again and took part of his head off with a last salvo.

"Raven!" Pope shouted. He and Chen rose to run. The grenade inside the barn exploded.

RAVEN WATCHED one of the last gunners pitch over, dead. The other tossed a grenade before Pope nailed him. The grenade sailed through the doorway.

"Grenade!" Ellison shouted.

Raven lost sight of the explosive in the thick smoke. His eyes stung, watered. The temperature was going up by the second. He was sweating through his uniform and tried not to cough. The others did cough. They needed to get out. The grenade might have landed next to any of them and they wouldn't know until the blast went off.

The blast jolted Raven, shrapnel tore at his camo, the concussion slamming his body.

"Everybody up!" Raven shouted. He wasn't sure they heard him. He rose, coughing now, trying to see through teary eyes. He needed to find Ellison, Starkey, and Marshall. He found Ellison first, the big man on his feet. Marshall found them next, and Starkey leaned against the bomb expert for support.

"He can't see!" Marshall shouted.

The scorching heat didn't let up as they ran for the hole in the wall. Pope and Chen waited beyond.

12

HOT SPOTS STILL SMOLDERED. MEN WITH WATER TANKS strapped to their back roamed the destroyed farm. They squirted any potential re-ignition points with thin streams of water.

A black Mercedes pulled up. Sevilla and Meza stepped out. Behind the four-door, in a black GMC Suburban, four cartel troops exited. They gunners fanned out to stand on the side of or behind Sevilla. Weapons ready. Eyes scanning for targets. Eager for a kill.

Sevilla stared at the blackened farm, the charred ruins of the barns and buildings. He shook his head. The massive litter of spent shell casings glistened in the overhead sun.

"Who would do this?" he asked Meza. "Panadero?"

"Not his style," Meza said. "Plus, we'd have heard a whisper if he was going to."

"This makes no sense."

"It does to somebody," Meza pointed out.

Everybody at the mansion had heard the battle. It took a few moments to determine where the fight was, but Sevilla had a greater concern on his mind. They had to protect the crop. He sent men to fight the blaze with the unique fire suppression system he built into his farms. The destruction of the processing buildings rendered the system useless. He sent a water tanker, from his property, kept for such emergencies. The tanker crew battled the blaze with a massive high-pressure water assault. But they hadn't been able to save the crop.

"This means nothing," Sevilla said. "This is a nuisance. It won't stop *anything*."

Meza tugged on Sevilla's right arm. "I'm getting a bad feeling. We need to go back."

"What do you mean?"

"You're right. It makes no sense. Except to get you out in the open."

"You don't—"

"Let's go. *Now*."

Sevilla followed Meza back to the Mercedes. The gun crew returned to the Suburban. The driver behind the wheel of the Mercedes made a U-turn and the Suburban followed. A short dirt road led back to the paved road leading to and from the mansion. Meza told the driver to step on the gas. The driver did; the engine surged and the scenery raced by. The Suburban kept up without a problem, thanks to its big V8. The SUV remained half a car length from the rear bumper.

But they had to slow for the curve.

The driver eased off the gas and applied a small amount of brake pressure. The Mercedes reduced speed, and his practiced hands turned the wheel. As the car came out of the turn, the driver straightened. He moved his foot to the gas pedal and—

The road exploded. Flame and chunks of asphalt flew into the air. Armored or not, the chunks smashed with authority into the front of the Mercedes. A bigger chunk pounded the windshield and bent the roof line.

The tires screamed as the Mercedes continued forward, the front end smashed. It began to twist sideways as the vehicle neared the hole blown in the road. The car struck the hole, flipped over, and flipped again and again. Metal crunched. Glass shattered. Bodies inside were tossed around like clothes in a dryer. The car flipped off the roadway into the forest where it came to a sudden and destructive smash against a tree.

The Suburban screeched to a halt. The gunmen piled out— the driver joined them, a fifth man with a gun. They rushed to the wreckage without checking around them. The side of the road erupted with five streams of deadly automatic gun fire. Four rifles popped in rapid succession. The heavier caliber of a machine gun thumped out its messengers of 5.56 and 7.62mm death. The cartel gunners danced and spun as the bullets tore red fleshy chunks out of their bodies. They all collapsed on the ground with finality, and the gun fire stopped.

Raven and his men reloaded quickly. Pope, still at the M-60, left the machine gun in place and grabbed the HK416 from the sling around his back. Raven led the way to the Mercedes. They didn't approach in a line. The team spread out with a few feet of space between them in case somebody in the car had a gun.

Raven took the lead, stepping over fallen tree limbs, crunching dried leaves. Somebody whimpered, cried in pain; they reached the car. A man Raven did not recognize was trying to pull Sevilla out of the Mercedes. Raven fired a burst from the HK. The gun thundered. The salvo jolted the other man and he slammed into the car before collapsing. Sevilla screamed at Raven, unintelligible rage. Raven stared at him coldly. The big-time drug dealer was trapped and nobody was coming to save him and he knew it. So much for his big empire, his invincibility. *We all get it eventually,* Raven thought to himself. *Don't think you're any better.*

He gestured for Ellison to drag away the other body. Ellison did so. Sevilla continued to yell, but he didn't beg. He was cursing his killers all the way to the end. Raven fired again. Sevilla stopped shouting, stopping moving.

Pope confirmed the driver was dead, too.

"Back to camp and let's get out of here," Raven said. "Job's done."

Pope and Chen went back for the M-60, then re-joined the team. They marched quietly but swiftly through the forest.

"CAN'T BLAME THE GUY," Ellison said, "for not going out like a little bitch."

Ellison walked near Raven as they headed for the camp. Raven had already radioed for the extraction team to come and get them. It would feel good to tell Kendrick Ward the mission was a success. It wouldn't bring back his kid. Sevilla's replacement would take over the command chair faster than they anticipated. But maybe Ward would feel he'd reached the closure he required. And Raven didn't mind have two million bucks filling his coffers.

"May we all be so bold when our time comes," Raven said.

"You think it'll be soon?"

"You never know. I should have been killed a dozen times over the years. Something keeps me going."

"Guardian angel?"

"More like a curse." Raven laughed. "Whatever it is, someday I know it's not going to be there."

"But not now," Ellison said.

"No, not now."

They arrived at the base camp, hurried to pack up, and began the second leg of their march to the extraction zone. Their pickup site was ten miles north of the camp. The forest grew thicker. They moved slower. Couldn't be helped —the obstacles in their way were much larger. They also paused to see if they were being followed, doubling back on their own trail looking for signs of pursuit. There was none. If the Sevilla estate knew of the death of their boss, they were reacting without sending out a search party.

When the team reached the grassy clearing, they stopped to rest with sighs of relief.

But Raven remained on his feet. He scanned the sky with binoculars.

"Any sign?" asked Starkey. He came up alongside Raven, in much better shape than when they'd carried him out of the drug farm. Too much smoke had stung his eyes to the point he couldn't keep them open. Raven had feared the worst, but a few dabs with a wet washcloth saved the day.

"Not yet. I guess we're early."

"Figured we'd have been late with the delays."

"Here it comes."

Starkey alerted the rest of the team. Every man stood with his pack and weapons, but the rifles weren't on safe. They remained fully loaded, and each merc kept up a security scan of the area around them. In case of a Sevilla counterattack. They knew cartel troops hadn't followed, but they also knew better than to relax. There would be no celebration until they were well away from Colombia and back in the United States. With cold beers and fat wallets.

The chopper appeared over the tree line on the opposite end of the field. The team took up security positions, weapons turned the way they'd come, to the side. Raven popped a canister of yellow smoke and tossed it ahead. The yellow plume blew thick as it hissed from the canister. It was a signal to the pilot to exercise caution with his landing. Raven couldn't promise zero incoming threats. They didn't see any, but an enemy who knew the area better than they could hide until the last second. Raven and his crew had to run into the open to reach the chopper. They'd be vulnerable for longer than he was comfortable with.

The chopper gave Raven a flashback to his army days. It was the UH-1 Iroquois, aka a "Huey". The helicopter immortalized by a long period of service in the US military and elsewhere. The chopper bore a green shade but no other markings except an ID number on the side.

The chopper came closer, the rotor wash creating a wind storm. The trees shook and leaves rustled. The grass flattened as the chopper neared the ground. Then Raven frowned as the Huey spun on its center axis. The starboard side door was wide open. A machine gun sat on a swivel mount with a man behind the gun. And he aimed the gun at Raven and the other mercenaries.

"Holy shit!" somebody behind him shouted.

"Down!" Raven shouted back. He hit the ground.

The machine gun spit flame as it chugged steel death at unsuspecting targets.

13

RAVEN SHOULDER-ROLLED INTO THE GROUND, GRUNTING AS debris smacked his body. But he had to get out of the way. The swarm of machine gun fire zipped over their position. Tree trunks popped, twigs fell and scattered, somebody—more than one somebody—screamed. Raven dared not look. He kept rolling for deeper cover. He finally stopped and shouldered his HK to point through a gap between two branches. He started firing. The HK bucked against his shoulder. He directed his shots at the gunner behind the machine gun. One scored, and the gunner slumped against the weapon. The shooting stopped.

Five more gunmen piled out of the chopper and rushed the tree line, firing as they ran. More rounds chopped through the foliage. The gunners ran halfway from the chopper, then dropped flat. Raven soon saw why. The chopper rotated on its axis again, the nose pointing toward them. The rocket pods on either side of the Huey loomed large. Raven fired the HK empty and put his face in the dirt and hands over the back of his neck. There was nothing more he could do.

The rockets flashed from either pod, streaks of fire and smoke trailing behind them.

THE ROCKETS HIT WITH FEROCITY. The ground churned with one intense explosion after another. Trees fell. Men fell. The mercenaries never had a chance, never had time to scream. Parts of them flew one way, parts of them flew another. Tree trunks toppled on corpses and the rocket blasts ceased. The gunners from the Huey moved forward. They kept their rifles at the ready.

The thick smoke from the rocket impacts didn't hang around long. The wind generated by the Huey's rotor wash swept it away. All it left behind was the stink of death and splintered tree trunks.

The five gunners didn't bother to sift through the carnage. They confirmed the dead by their body parts. The rockets had torn up the space to where a careful examination wasn't warranted. The mercenaries were dead. They'd been ordered to confirm as such, and they agreed they'd accomplished the mission. Each man hurried back to the waiting chopper. But this time they held their weapons more casually than before. They climbed back into the helicopter. Two helped the dead machine gunner into the cabin. Such losses were part of the game. The Huey pilot raised the chopper over the tree line, turned in the direction they'd come, and tipped the nose forward.

The chopper left behind only the deathly silence of the slaughter zone.

RAVEN FELT the heavy weight on his back as he came to.

He couldn't get up. He could barely move side-to-side. But he managed to get his hands from the back of his neck and tried to push up against the weight. No go. He sank flat. His head hurt. He felt dizzy. He had no way to tell if he'd been wounded. Finally, he turned his head left and right to try and see what happened. A pair of tree trunks had fallen atop his position, but neither fell all the way to crush him. They'd stopped inches from doing so, held back by thick roots. He scooted left a few inches, then a few more. The path was clear on that side, and he slid out from under the crisscross. He crawled through forest debris, dragging his empty rifle with him. He rose to full height with his left arm above his head to push branches out of the way. One snapped back at his face; he ignored it. Dirt and broken leaves fell from his uniform; more dirt stained his pants and stuck to his boots. When he finally stood upright, he was unsteady, still dizzy. He leaned against a tree for support, and froze at the destruction only a few yards away.

The mass of destroyed foliage, fallen and broken trunks, churned ground, and bloody pieces of what had once been his team lay before him. There was no sense checking for survivors. Nobody could have survived the attack. How he had made he didn't know. Ellison had asked about a guardian angel; Raven wanted to know why it only spared him. He wanted to know what to do now that he was alone.

"You think this is a set-up."

He'd said the words to Pope back at their training camp. When the main topic of conversation was their doubts about Ward and his sources.

Raven's legs gave out and he hit the ground hard. He wanted to lay there and die. Why had he survived? He checked his body for wounds, saw none, so where was the pain coming from?

His team was dead.

Ward was dirty. He'd used them for a purpose and used another team to get rid of them once they accomplished the purpose.

Why? *What for?*

Raven raised his head. A noise. Voices, a whistle. A dog barked.

He slapped a new mag into the HK and chambered a round. Sevilla's forces were coming to investigate the rocket attack. He scrambled over mounds of dirt and debris to grab for somebody's torso. He recognized who it belonged to— Starkey. Fireplug. *Sorry, pal.* Starkey's chest pack with spare mags and grenades remained intact. Raven grabbed the mags and grenades and stuffed them in every available pocket. Blood smeared the items, stained his hands. He didn't know who the blood belonged to, but he'd kill whoever spilled it. He'd kill Ward for setting them up.

The dog barked again.

Raven reversed his steps and let adrenaline provide the fuel he needed. Without it, he'd have stayed in place. He ran hard and jumped and ducked and tried to put distance between him and the on-coming cartel troops. But they had a dog. A dog who would track his scent. His only hope for escape was to make it back to the stream where they'd camped and lose the scent in the water. He had to move fast. *Hurry. They're getting closer...*

14

RAVEN BREATHED HARD AS HE RAN. HE STUMBLED OVER obstacles, kept getting hit in the face by low-slung branches. But he maintained his momentum. The Sevilla party wouldn't inspect the carnage for more than a few moments. The dog, or dogs, would immediately pick up his scent. They'd know somebody survived and was on the loose.

He ran as hard as he dared, even when the ground began to slope upward. He breathed hard and lungs strained. His legs hurt. Sweat dripped into his eyes. He didn't stop. To stop meant death. When he heard the dog begin to bark in rapid succession, he knew death wasn't far away. The dog had sniffed him out. He had to keep going. He had to—

His right foot smacked a tree root. Raven tumbled forward. He hit hard and rolled to the right, out of control, brush and branches swishing around him. He stopped and groaned. Pain flared through him. But he couldn't stay put.

Raven ran hard. He knocked low-hanging branches out of the way. His boots crunched leaves beneath him. He didn't care about the noise. His rest had let the enemy get closer, and they weren't far behind. They were also in better shape than he was. He had no idea how many he faced. He knew they had one dog. The dog was a force multiplier. An ace in the hole. They'd never lose track of him as long as the dog's nose found his scent.

He zig-zagged until the forest became less dense, and his legs burned with strain as he stated up a slope. The dog barked louder now. He decided running was pointless—he'd only run out of gas and die tired. He needed to make a stand now.

A half-trunk of about six feet in diameter, hollowed out by time and nature, provided a hiding spot. He didn't climb into the bowl. To do so was sure suicide. He flattened behind it and pulled a grenade from his vest. Yanking the pin, he held the explosive tightly. The pursuit force made more noise than he had.

Leaves jostled as they moved through the ground growth, the dog growling. Another Doberman. Raven waited till they broke through the same clearing he'd found and started up. There were six of them. All toted automatic rifles with kill fury plastered over their faces. Raven tossed the grenade. It plopped on the ground in front of the man holding the leash. He screamed for his men to get down.

The blast disintegrated the man and flung the Doberman into the air. The animal bounced on landing and stopped in a heap on the second touchdown.

Raven fired the HK, one three-round burst, then another. Two of the gunners dropped, their chests sprouting red entry holes before the high-velocity slugs punched out their backside. Return fire kicked up dirt around Raven and snapped bark from the trunk. The hard bits landed on Raven's back. He tossed another grenade. Somebody yelled. Return fire ceases. Raven ran as the explosive shook the ground.

He angled down the slope. He reached the point where he thought he was parallel with the surviving pursuit party. He slid to the ground and rolled onto his belly with the HK416 at the ready. He waited as the smoke cleared.

Only two remained. They yelled to each other as they started climbing, heading for the hollow trunk. Raven waited some more. They fired into his former position, but stopped abruptly when they realized he wasn't there. As they turned to head back into the overgrowth, Raven squeezed the trigger. His first burst struck the neck of one, a shower of red striking his partner. Raven fired again and the last man went down. Both tumbled down the slope a short distance before sliding to a stop.

Raven let out a breath. He didn't move. He kept his muzzle pointed at the danger zone and waited to see if he'd missed any. He used the downtime to reload. Pocketing the partially-spent magazine, he continued to scan.

No further danger.

Raven eased to his feet. His body ached. His mind raced with anxious thoughts. He'd slain the pursuit force, but they weren't the men he wanted to kill. He wanted to kill the men in the Huey. He wanted to kill the man who sent them. His team should still be with him. They should have been in the air, on their way home. Instead, only he survived and the others were body parts strewn across the forest floor.

Raven continued his upward hike, but at a slower pace. The ground eventually flattened out, and he continued a cautious pace. The cartel might be anywhere looking for the ones responsible for killing Sevilla. He still wanted to reach their former camp. Why, he didn't know. There was no safety there. But it felt like home—and had been for their time in-country. He'd find the camp, and the stream, and decide what to do after he had a chance to rest.

If he had the chance.

Along the way, Raven got lost and had to backtrack,

change course, and find his bearings. When he finally reached the former camp, he collapsed against a tree.

He was alone.

It seemed like he was always alone. And he shouldn't have been.

He touched the locket under his shirt. The ghosts of battles past were with him, providing overwatch, but yet he still wondered why he'd survived. The stream trickled and provided the soundtrack to his thoughts. They were dark thoughts. It would be so easy to end it here. One bullet through the head and done. Enough of the pain. Enough of the war without end. But deep down, he knew it wasn't the answer. He had to survive to fight the battles others weren't able to. Right now, his former teammates had no way to fight back, to avenge their betrayal.

But Raven could.

He had no maps of the area. Ellison and Pope had carried the intel. He watched the stream and decided the best course was to follow where it led. He might find a village where he could get help, though the idea held no appeal. Anybody he came in contact with would turn him over to the cartel—any cartel, not necessarily Sevilla's. But he didn't know what else to do. He might get lucky.

Raven followed the stream, and when he saw the water deepen, he stepped into the flow. It was better to be carried than walk. He floated on the surface and let the current carry him along. The shock of the cold water revived him somewhere, woke him up, kept him alert. Somewhere along the way he passed out, and began to choke. Snorting water, he thrashed about to reach the right edge, where he lay gasping. Eventually he passed out again. His last thought before the blanket of darkness fell over him was that it might be nice not to wake up...

15

BRADLEY PATEL OF THE DEA HUNG UP THE PHONE AND frowned. His colleague Hollie Chandler, who studied a map on the office wall, turned to him.

"Well?" she said.

"Some sort of happening at Sevilla's," Patel said. "It's odd."

"What happened?"

"Either he's dead or there's some sort of battle going on. Somebody torched a grow field, and there's been an explosion on the road to Sevilla's mansion. That's all our source knows right now."

Hollie folded her arms. "Panadero?"

"Can't be. He doesn't have the US connection yet. His power isn't consolidated. Making a move on Sevilla now doesn't make sense."

"And we haven't hurt him enough to make him jump early," she said.

They worked out of a gray concrete building in Bogota. They were part of the DEA's rotation of agents who helped the Colombian government fight the cartels. They worked with officers of the Colombian National Police and Prosecutor's Office. Each member of their team was hand-picked after an exhaustive vetting process. They didn't want any cartel plants on the staff. But problems persisted. The cartels tried to recruit members as moles. Constant vigilance and checking on staff remained top priority.

One could make the case the US government's pledge to fight the drug trade often resembled a hollow promise. The US spent close to $500 million dollars a year on DEA efforts in Colombia. Publicly, there wasn't always evidence of the investment providing a decent return. Even the drug fighters wondered if their blood, sweat, and contributed to the end of the "War on Drugs". But they stayed at their post because often times the answer was a resounding yes. Other times? They tried not to think about those other times.

Patel and Chandler were on a six-month rotation. The current target of the task force was cartel boss Antonio Panadero. Panadero had a plan to expand his operation into the United States; Martin Sevilla stood in his way. Sevilla already controlled the territory Panadero wanted. But, according to their source, somebody removed Sevilla from the equation.

"We need more information," Hollie said. "When will your contact call back?"

Patel shrugged. "As soon as he has more. Could be an hour, could be—"

"Next week, yeah, yeah," she said.

A knock in the open doorway turned their attention to a new arrival. He was a Colombian officer in a green uniform. "They're ready," the man said.

"Thank you, Lieutenant," Hollie said. "Give us two minutes."

The officer nodded and departed.

Patel waited for Hollie to say something. She was the more outspoken of the two.

"Sevilla being dead isn't a bad thing," she said.

"No," he agreed. "But I don't like mystery. We have no idea what's going on over there."

"Don't let it detract from our main goal, which is Panadero, which means, if he's involved, we'll solve this mystery soon enough."

Patel nodded.

"Let's go."

"We still have a minute." He grinned.

"I'll do all the talking if you're too shy," she said. Hollie laughed. They walked down the hall together.

HOLLIE CHANDLER WAS surprised she found anything to laugh at whatsoever.

A personal phone call, the previous evening, shook her foundation. She didn't know what to do.

Her husband phoned with bad news. Robert reported catching their son, Todd, drinking. Todd was 13-years-old. Hollie's father had brought a bottle of scotch last Thanksgiving. Robert didn't drink scotch, so it sat in the liquor cabinet. Then Robert found the amount of scotch getting lower. There was only one other person in the house. Robert confronted Todd, who admitted to taking sips. He started crying when his father asked further questions. Robert needed her back home, ASAP, because they needed to address the problem together. Hollie had two more months on her rotation; she was also afraid to go home. It ran in the genes. She'd started drinking early, too, before AA saved her life. She knew from the program that running from problems wasn't a way to solve them. But if her son was going to travel down the same path she'd traversed, they had bigger problems than she wanted to admit.

Even Patel had told her to get on a flight and go home.

She stubbornly refused. For now. There was too much in Bogota unfinished, projects *she'd* started. She had to see matters further along and then she could go home. Another few days. Maybe.

Panadero was her primary target. She wanted to see him taken down.

But how could she work to "save" the world from the drug problem when she couldn't even protect one child at home?

She pushed the thoughts out of her mind. She and Patel entered the briefing room to address the troops on new developments.

They were closer to nailing Panadero than ever before.

PATEL STOOD to the side as Hollie began the briefing. Colombian officers in green uniforms filled the seats. DEA personnel wore suits and stood near the back wall.

She commanded the room for sure, he decided. Despite the news from the night before. He didn't understand why she wasn't going home. She was stubborn. Too stubborn for her own good.

"We may finally have our best lead to taking down Antonio Panadero," she announced. Patel pulled down the projection screen behind her. Hollie hit keys on a laptop. The computer was connected to a screen projector, and a man's face appeared on the pull-down.

Hollie continued.

"This man is Saúl Elvira. He lives here in Bogota, and he's an accountant. But not just any accountant. Elvira is the personal number cruncher for Antonio Panadero. He's been operating his own business for over twenty years, and never had anything to do with the cartels until five years ago.

"Elvira was caught embezzling from clients," Hollie continued. "Panadero made the charges go away in return for keeping the cartel's books. But as I said, he's our best lead. He has more inside information on Panadero's operation than anybody short of Panadero himself. If we can turn him, it will be everything we need to bring Panadero down once and for all."

She paused to let the words sink in. The audience took notes. Pens scratched on paper; somebody coughed. Hollie continued.

"Our plan for right now is to keep Elvira under surveillance. We want to map his movements, see who he meets. We suspect Panadero will meet Elvira in the coming days. The two meet twice a year to go over financials. Nobody will make any overt moves no matter what you see. Observe and report. Understood?"

The briefing ended with a few questions, and Patel shook his head as he watched. Nobody would know she had more on her mind than work; it bothered him she hid her problems so well.

16

RAVEN JERKED AWAKE. FROM A NIGHTMARE. BUT LIKE MANY nightmares, upon opening his eyes the vision vanished. He'd seen darkness, heard screaming and heart-wrenching heavy sobs. He remained still, heart beating fast, and then faster, because he sat up and looked around. He wasn't where he last remembered. He wasn't on the edge of the stream wishing he was dead.

A tent. A plain, non-descript tent. Sleeping bag. Foam pillow. His gear stacked in a corner, including weapons. He was only in his skivvies, with the sterling silver locket remaining around his neck. He grasped it as if holding on for life. *Okay. I'm...somewhere not dead.*

Voices. Several voices, a mix of male and female, people busy. The zipper at the front of the tent was closed. Mesh-covered openings on either side of him allowed air circulation. They also allowed him to peek outside and see where the voices originated.

People passed by. A battered pick-up sat half out of sight. He smelled food cooking.

Where am I?

The front of the tent rustled as the zipper holding the flaps closed moved up. Raven grabbed for the .45 near his pack, and jacked back the slide. The chambered round flew out as another replaced it. But a different instinct than survival took over. He upped the thumb safety and lowered the muzzle. Somehow, he knew he wasn't in danger, but couldn't explain how he knew. The zipper reached the top and hands entered to part the flaps. Raven looked at the face of a young women as she smiled at him.

"Good morning. Or afternoon, rather," she said. "I thought you might be awake by now."

She was white, American; blue-eyed blonde. Thin tank top, jeans; no makeup or jewelry.

"You can put the gun away. It's okay. We're just a bunch of church nerds hanging out in the forest."

"Church nerds?"

"Missionaries," she said. "We're from the US."

"And you're roughing it," Raven said.

"Sort of. We got a propane stove." She laughed. "Not really *roughing* it, by usual standards."

"Where am I?"

"You want to get dressed? Dip in the water a bit?" She half-smiled. "It's not every day we find a man half-dead and manage to save him. A lot of people would like to say hello. Also, put the gun away? Doesn't bother me but I know it'll make a few others nervous. They didn't want us to bring them back. You know, with the rest of you."

Raven lowered the pistol. "Please tell me who you are."

"Hi, I'm Kaylee." She stuck out a hand. Raven shook. She was thin and bony and her hand was warm. She wore her hair in a pony tail, but a few strands rebelled and dangled behind her ears and in front of her face.

"Sam," he said.

"Were you part of an army unit? Got lost or something?"

"Or something."

"You're white so we know you're not cartel. We've seen a few of them."

"I'm not cartel material, no."

"It wouldn't matter. Leaving you in the stream wasn't an option for us. You know the story of the Good Samaritan? We had to help you. But it's nice to know you're not a bad guy."

"Sure," Raven said.

"You don't say much, do you?"

"I'm mostly naked and in a strange place, Kaylee. Would you say much till you knew more?"

She forced a laugh. "Get dressed and come on out. We have food cooking and my father will want to see you, too."

Another woman called, "Hey, Kaylee!"

"Oops! They caught me. Gotta go." She grinned and zipped the flaps closed. "See you in a minute." Raven heard her shoes crunch on the ground as she walked away. She called out, "He's awake!" as she joined her friends.

Raven let out a breath. He stared at his gun a moment, then found the ejected cartridge in the corner. Buttoning out the magazine, he fed the round back into the mag and slapped the mag in place. He left the gun cocked and locked. Raven rooted through his pack for his spare street clothes, pulled them on, and then found a pair of tennis shoes. They'd flattened with all the crap packed on top of them. He jammed his hand into each to put them back in shape, and slipped them onto his sore feet. The shock of his new location wore off, and the throbs of pain throughout his body returned. He examined himself, but saw no wounds. Only dark bruises. Many dark bruises. He'd managed to survive the slaughter unscathed while good men had died. He felt depressed. The feeling hung heavy, especially in his mind.

It was his job to save people, not lose them.

Like he'd lost his team when they'd faced the greatest danger of the mission. Betrayal by the man who hired them.

He'd see Kendrick Ward again. One on one, with a weapon in his hand. He'd see Ward again no matter how high the cost might climb.

RAVEN EASED out of the tent and scanned the area. His eyes were nervous, darting back and forth; his lips made a flat line. He was afraid to step forward.

Footsteps on his left. He turned. Kaylee smiled big as she led another man to him. The man was taller than her, older, and examined Raven with eyes used to searching for threats.

"Here he is, Daddy," Kaylee said. "Sam, this is my father, Travis."

"Hello," the man said. He had a deep voice. "Travis Gray. I'm a doctor in California." He held out a hand. Raven shook. He was heavier than his daughter, looked middle-aged. He wore jeans and an untucked button-down shirt. "I'm the leader of our little group," he continued. "We're on a medical mission. Visiting villages and places where they don't have doctors. We pass out medicine, do vaccinations, check-ups, all that."

"Kaylee called you all church nerds."

He laughed. "Makes sense. We're with the Concord Bible Church. Ever been to California?"

"Few times."

"Nice. So, um—"

"How did I end up in the stream half-dead?"

He laughed nervously.

Raven didn't want to talk about the circumstances leading to his discovery. He said instead, "I'll tell you once I've woken up a little more. Why don't you show me around?"

"Follow me," Dr. Gray told him.

17

MORE TENTS DOTTED THE SMALL CAMP GROUND. THEY WERE in a clearing near a stream and within a short distance of a paved road. There were fifteen people in the missionary group, mostly married couples. Kaylee and two girls her age shared one tent. Her father was the only occupant of his own. As he showed Raven around, Raven noticed he didn't wear a wedding ring.

"We have several trucks and the van," Dr. Gray explained. "Various medical supplies, medicine, all that. We're reaching out to towns and villages where they don't have ready access to medical care. You'd be surprised how many there are."

Raven disagreed. He knew the score. But he didn't want to argue the point too hard. He didn't have the energy to do so. The walking helped get the kinks out of his body, though. The fresh air was nice. The heat? Not so much.

Gray showed him the supplies in the beds of each truck. The van was a mobile doctor's office with other medical equipment. Raven's unfocused mind glossed over the details. He saw items he recognized, and it was enough to convince him. They didn't need to prove anything to him. He knew that wasn't the reason for the tour. This was a "getting to know you" tour. The group leader wanted one-on-one time with Raven before anybody else got involved. Raven also noticed he hadn't bothered, nor did anybody crowd him. The group understood they had to stay back until the doctor gave the okay.

Gray explained most of his group had medical training. They were paramedics, emergency room nurses; Gray was the only full-fledged doctor. Kaylee and her friends, the youngest members of the group, documented the trip with video gear. Gray said his daughter intended to assemble a "documentary" of the footage. The movie would promote their efforts and help them collect financial support. Money, he told Raven, was always short for goodwill missions such as this.

"Why?" Raven asked.

"Sometimes the church is so focused on doing big things, we forget the small things have an impact, too. The big ministries can get all the money they need. Small stuff like this? We have to try harder."

They wandered to the food area. Two burly men worked the propane grill cooking sliced meat and chicken. The grill was hot; the two men sweated. They wore soaked bandannas around their heads. Two women chopped vegetables. The heat of the grill didn't bother them. Gray asked Raven if he felt like eating. Raven's stomach rumbled at the smell of the seasoned meat; he said yes. Gray handed him a plate from a stack. Raven lined up with the rest. He exchanged polite hellos and nods, but nobody tried to talk to him.

Kaylee and her two friends glanced at Raven more than the others. He caught them once or twice. They retreated with embarrassed grins and bursts of laughter.

The server gave him three slices of meat and three pieces of boneless chicken, veggies, and a bottle of water. Gray led

Raven to a spot away from the rest. They sat down on warm grass.

"Forgive my daughter," Gray said.

"I'm a curiosity," Raven said.

"She's seventeen." He and Raven started eating. "Her mother used to love trips like this."

"Is she back home?"

Gray shook his head. Raven realized he shouldn't have asked. He knew the answer before the doctor provided it.

"She died two years ago. We're still...adjusting."

"I'm sorry," Raven told him.

He watched Gray eat a moment. The man's mind was now elsewhere, thinking of a lost wife and lost mother. Raven identified with him. Another member of the exclusive club. He didn't dare ask how his wife had passed. It wasn't his business, anyway.

Gray was solidly built and had broad shoulders. Thick hair and mustache, both touched with specks of white. He looked too old to have a daughter as young as Kaylee. Raven figured she came along late in the marriage but they were happy to have her nonetheless.

Gray swallowed and drank some water. He addressed Raven again.

"You, on the other hand, could use an examination. I checked you out while you were unconscious, and you didn't appear badly injured. How do you feel?"

"Aches and pains."

"Anything else?"

Raven shook his head.

"You've been banged up enough," Gray said, "that you'd know if you were seriously hurt somehow. I saw the scars."

Raven nodded. The scars covered his body. He saw them every time he stood naked in front of a mirror. He saw the scars and wondered how he survived.

Guardian angel?

Curse?

He didn't want to think about it.

"It's mostly mental strain right now, Doctor."

"Can you tell me what happened? Are you US army or..."

"Let's just say *or* and leave it alone. I was with a larger group, something happened, and only I escaped."

"My goodness...that's..."

"More than I should have told you, and I don't mean to burden you. But it's how I wound up almost drowning. I got to the edge of the stream before passing out."

Raven tried to stop talking but the words leaped out before he realized what he was saying.

"For a bit, I didn't care if I drowned or not. Know what I mean?"

"I do," Gray said. "I understand. There's no shame here, Sam."

Raven blinked. He'd forgotten he told the other man his name. He also wasn't used to hearing "Sam" spoken by any companion. Most of them only called him "Raven."

"I shouldn't have—"

"No, it's fine," Gray said. "It helps to talk about these things. And I *do* understand. If it hadn't been for my daughter, when my wife died—"

Raven nodded again. They understood each other far too well.

But he didn't want to get personal. He'd deal with his issues in his own time, not by involving a doctor he barely knew. Or he wouldn't. Not every issue needed sorting. Some deserved to stay buried. Like how he received one or two of his scars.

"You're a long way from civilization out here," Raven said. "You have any trouble from—"

"The cartels? No. It's interesting how many of them actually call themselves practicing Catholics. When you bring God into the equation, they suddenly find lines they aren't willing to cross."

"Interesting. Even if this isn't a Catholic group?"

"It's not like that. They know who we represent. They give us the room to work. But," Gray continued, "we do have to watch out for, I guess you'd call them, *bandits*. They'd like our supplies, stuff they can turn around and sell. Luckily, we haven't seen much of them, so far, this trip."

"Here's to luck holding out." Raven raised his water bottle. Gray smiled and "clinked" his bottle to Raven's. They drank.

18

KAYLEE GRAY WATCHED HER FATHER TALK TO THE MAN NAMED Sam and wondered what they were saying to each other. Knowing her father, he wasn't doing a generic get-to-know session. He was asking real questions. Whether Sam answered the questions was anybody's guess, but he seemed to be talking almost as much as her father. He wasn't playing the strong silent bit.

She sat on a piece of cardboard to protect her jeans from getting dirty. Her two friends, Carrie and Vicki, sat likewise; the other adults thought it was silly. It probably was. They had to make sure they kept the dirty side of the cardboard on the ground. If they mixed it up, the whole effort was moot. The three girls knew each other from their church youth group. They'd been inseparable friends since junior high.

"Stop staring," Carrie told Kaylee. Carrie was the police officer of the group. She made sure they didn't go off the rails. "It's not appropriate."

Kaylee grinned and ate a bite of chicken. "You should have seen him in the tent."

Vicki stifled a smile; Carrie frowned. "Don't encourage

her," she told Vicki. To Kaylee: "Remember what we're here for, okay? Besides, your father doesn't look too thrilled with this guy being here."

"He always looks like that," Kaylee said. "It means he's thinking."

"What do you think he's thinking?" Vicki asked.

"I don't know," Kaylee said. "Dad never tells. He's hard to communicate with sometimes."

Carrie said, "When we do our video tomorrow, let's make sure we keep this guy off camera, okay?"

"Kaylee can get some private shots later," Vicki said, grinning.

"Well—" Kaylee began.

"Stop it," Carrie said. "You're both being gross and un-Christlike."

"Okay, *mom*," Vicki said.

Neither noticed Kaylee's smile fade a little.

"THANKS FOR LUNCH," Raven said, as he and Gray finished and stood. "If you don't mind, I'll go back to the tent for a bit."

"By all means." Gray collected the plates. They held onto their water bottles. "You need the rest."

"I'm not using somebody else's tent, am I?"

"No, it's a spare I brought along in case one of the crew had an issue or something."

"About my weapons—"

Gray waved him off. "There will be two or three who might be sensitive, but the rest you won't have a problem with. I don't mind having them here. You are capable of putting them to use, for sure. But...keep them on the QT, if you don't mind."

"Of course. And thank you for the hospitality."

"You're welcome, Sam."

"People usually call me *Raven*. It's my last name."

"You're welcome, Mr. Raven."

"No mister, just Raven."

Gray smiled. "You can call me anything you want except late for dinner."

Raven laughed a little. "See you in a bit. Are you pulling out of here tomorrow morning?"

"After breakfast. You're welcome to remain with us for a while."

"I think I will."

Raven made his way back to the spare tent and rested on top of the sleeping bag. He lay awake listening to the crew clean up and scolded himself for not lending a hand. Before he argued himself back outside to help, he dozed off again.

KAYLEE CAME to check on him around dinner time. He ate with the group, and joined the singing circle around a big fire. Somebody with a guitar led the singing, worship songs on the agenda for the evening. Raven wanted to know if the guitar player knew *Jail House Rock*. After a while the singing stopped, and Gray read from the Bible. Then they went around the circle discussing the passages. Raven listened without comment.

Later, Raven asked for a light. Kaylee brought him a battery-powered lantern-style light he placed off to the side. He found her watching; he told her unless she wanted to help clean his guns, she might want to find something else to do. She seemed a little hurt as she excused herself. Raven shook his head. The last thing he needed was a teenage girl following him around like a puppy.

He scrubbed the HK416 and took stock of his ammo. Six original mags; two were empty. Three of the magazines had blood stuck to them. Starkey's blood. They were the mags Raven had taken off Starkey's corpse. Or *part* of his corpse. Raven left the blood where it was. Soon the time would come where he used those mags. He wanted a reminder of why the man on the other end of the gun deserved what came out of the business end.

The Nighthawk Custom .45 was still clean, unused. Raven scrubbed it anyway and re-oiled the mechanism. He had two spare 10-round magazines, plus the 8-shot mag in the pistol—28 total. Seven full mags for the HK rifle—210 total. Not a lot. But he only needed to get out of the forest and into Bogota. He didn't need to fight another war. *Yet.* Raven was a firm believer that the only time to have too much ammo was when you were on fire or drowning. The lack of cartridges bothered him. He wasn't fighting another war, but he was going into the unknown with vulnerable people. Then again, any cartel thug or bandit who made an appearance would have his own gear to collect after.

He appreciated what Gray and his church group were doing, but he didn't think it was smart. Their *vulnerability* was the key problem. Sure, they had God's protection. But the possibility of danger and harassment remained high. They were also easy pickings for kidnappings and ransom demands. Their effort was admirable, but they were stupid. Gray thought cartel thugs would stand down in the name of Jesus and Mary; Raven doubted most would bother. There was no reasoning with killers, spiritually or otherwise. And cartel thugs were killers. Nothing more, nothing less. Raven had his way of dealing with them; let God take over when they were dead. Raven's job was to arrange the face-to-face meeting.

Ward's briefing hadn't included anything about bandits.

What else had he left out? Raven had no idea what they might face when they broke camp next day. He wanted to keep his weapons out of sight, but available. The least he could do to repay the missionaries was to act as their armed escort going forward. Until he was himself again. And ready to deal with Kendrick Ward.

19

RAVEN PULLED UP THE TENT STAKES THE NEXT MORNING. HE had no choice but to don the combat vest and sling his rifle. He kept the pistol tucked in the waistband of his jeans in an IWB holster. So much for "on the QT." He stayed away from the bulk of the group and tried not to be conspicuous.

The van and trucks departed the camp at an easy pace, reaching the road only to increase speed to near 40 mph. The drivers saw no need to go faster, especially since everybody not in the van rode in the open backs of the trucks. Raven sat in the last truck in the line, where the people with him said little to him but much to each other. He didn't mind. One of the men asked if he was part of a special ops unit. Raven only shook his head. It would have been futile to say more. If the group thought he was some sort of special asset, it might help them warm up.

The convoy followed the winding two-lane road without incident. He had no idea which part of Colombia they were in, or how far, or close, they were to the Sevilla property. And what was happening inside the house since the big boss's death?

Then he remembered...

No. Not right now.

The whole operation might have been a small part of a bigger plan. What did Ward hope to gain? Why ambush the team he assembled? The betrayal made no sense, but only because Raven lacked key details. There was no denying the fact Ward's daughter was a victim of drugs. Nobody can plant such information in a public source on the off-hand chance a mercenary would see it. The overdose and death *happened*. But Ward wasn't honest about his true agenda. Did he need Sevilla out of the way for another reason? Did the people he did *business* with, and used Zac Fox as a go-between, required Sevilla's removal?

Another question. Assuming Ward was a patsy, did he even *know* about the ambush?

There was much he need to learn. To go charging back into New Jersey with guns blazing wouldn't help anybody if Ward wasn't the one responsible. He had to learn the truth before firing a shot. But once he did engage, he didn't plan to miss. There were five good men to avenge. He'd carry the message they couldn't.

The convoy pulled to a stop in a small town Raven didn't catch the name of. It looked like a place out of the old American Wild West. Main street lined with businesses and, especially, stores for agricultural products. The farm land he'd seen entering the area looked extensive. And none of it grown for drugs. The convoy drew a crowd right away. They'd parked in front of the local church, and were expected.

The church was typical of every Catholic house of worship throughout the world. The scale was much smaller, though. White walls, pointed turrets, stained glass. The church would be the main gathering place in town, second only to any saloon on the main street. Raven hadn't noticed one as they drove through, but that didn't mean anything. Every town had a saloon or two same as every town included a church without fail.

The priest came out to greet and talk to Gray. Gray and the priest embraced. This wasn't the first visit of the missionaries. Raven and the others waited; the only ones to talk were Kaylee and her two friends. They had video cameras rolling, with Kaylee doing a stand-up description of the town. She knew more about the place than anybody else in the group, Raven decided. He watched from a distance.

Shortly, Gray and the priest shook hands then addressed the gathering crowd. The missionaries began unloading medical supplies. Gray set up his unit inside the van. Raven helped unload, then stayed behind the truck, out of sight. Word spread of their arrival, and the line formed almost as fast. One little girl brought her dog for a check-up. One of the missionaries with veterinarian training took that one. Raven did not know what they'd do if the dog needed something. They only carried medicine for people. But it was none of his business.

At least he told himself it wasn't. He knew it should have been his business. The whole effort should have been his business. But these were people of peace and he was a man of war. Not because he enjoyed fighting, but because somebody had to when others could not. People like Gray's group. There was a place for both of them at the table, be it the heavenly table with God at the head or an earthly incarnation. Right? But he wasn't sure how he fit. It didn't feel natural. He'd known plenty of Christians in his years of service who had no trouble making the distinction. But he had so much more blood to his name now, he wondered if he belonged at all.

Raven took a deep breath and shook himself out of the

never-ending thought process. He'd never figure it out by himself.

Kaylee and the other two girls turned their cameras on the people lined up for check-ups. They videoed some of the missionaries, too. Several other priests and a handful of nuns helped with translating. They operated as a cohesive unit. Raven appreciated their coordination.

He noticed the girls avoided turning the camera on him. Either by their own choice or orders from her father, he didn't know. But staying away from the lens was a good move. He hid behind the truck he'd ridden in because he didn't want the locals disturbed by his rifle. This wasn't the place to cause a problem. Raven wished he had a better solution but the HK wouldn't fit in his pack unless he broke it down. Breaking down the weapon into parts would do him no good if trouble came calling.

He watched from the truck and nobody paid attention to him. And then he turned his head. Off to his left, on the wooden walkway in front of a feed store, two men observed. One of them looked at him and his weapon with his lips pressed together. He leaned toward his friend to say something. The friend only shook his head.

Raven turned back to the missionaries. His gut didn't tell him the two men were trouble, but he sensed a mountain of it was heading their way.

20

RAVEN HAD TROUBLE SLEEPING. HE LAY AWAKE TOO LONG AND became restless. He needed to stretch his legs a little.

He pulled on his jeans while inside the tent, found his shoes, and stepped out into the quiet night. A lot of snoring came from the tents around him. They were in another camp area between their last stop and the next stop. Gray alerted the crew they'd need to stock up on dwindling supplies at the next stop. They needed food and water and various other staples for the final leg of their trip. Then they'd wrap in Bogota at another church, and head for home. Raven only wanted to get to Bogota. The missionaries were as good a ride as any, and the rest was doing him good. His body ached less and less every day. But the burning desire to get to the bottom of the mystery remained top of mind. With pain no longer distracting him, he could focus on his next step full time.

The night was warm and the forest mysterious. Various critter sounds filled the air. But they stayed away from the big group of two-legged animals. The sounds comforted Raven. It meant there was no danger nearby. They'd have gone silent otherwise. He didn't know why his gut told him to be wary, but he knew not to argue. He hadn't liked the way the two men at the feed store watched the missionaries. The small-town folks hadn't done anything threatening or provided a reason to suspect them. He paced around his tent. He didn't want anything to happen to the group, and he was jumping at shadows. *Relax. If there's trouble, you'll deal with it. Don't make up a fight that doesn't exist.*

His head understood; his gut didn't.

He ducked back into his tent, grabbed the .45, and a spare ten-round magazine. He went out again.

The critters stopped making noise.

And the smell changed.

Raven's heart-rate kicked into overdrive. He found a tree and squatted low, listening. He scanned without looking directly at anything. He wanted his peripheral vision to sense movement foreign to the area. There was *something out there* and the critters were smart enough to go into silent mode.

Raven left the tree and dropped further back into the cover of the forest. He stretched out on the ground. Ten yards from the camp. He held the .45 tight and clicked off the thumb safety. No need to check the chamber. He knew a fat .45 hollow-point sat in the launch tube, ready to go. Ready to kill.

He waited and listened. His bare elbows sank into the dirt.

Then he heard the snaps and pops of foliage breaking under heavy boots.

The reason the critters went quiet.

Raven slipped his finger over the .45's trigger. Not long now.

The rustling and snapping grew louder, closer. Near him! To the left!

Raven turned his head a little. *There.* At the edge of his

vision. Three figures with automatic rifles silhouetted against the trees. They entered the camp and spread out. One carried a spotlight; he turned on the bright light, and Raven averted his eyes. The spotlight burned bright. *You dummies have ruined your night vision...*

Another pointed his rifle at the sky and let off a long burst. The rattled of gunfire breaking the silence even made Raven jump. It made everybody in the tents come alive, too.

Three more men entered from the other side, and one started yelling for the people in the tents to come out. He directed his men to bring them out; the goons attacked the tents. They ripped open zippered flaps, dragged out sleeping bags, hauled confused and disoriented missionaries to their feet. Everybody got shoved roughly into a group, then manhandled as the goons forced them into a line.

The younger girls were the last to join, and two men were having a good time with them. Their leader told them to stop fondling the young women. They shoved the girls into the line. Kaylee grabbed for her father. A goon pulled her away and punched her father in the belly. He shoved Kaylee into somebody else's grasp. Kaylee screamed as her father, doubled over, threw up onto the ground. The goon moved on.

Faces full of panic, chopped screams; Raven saw and heard all. He heard others muttering prayers. He had too much brush in front of him for a clear shot. He had to slowly move into a better position. He had an advantage. The spotlight made the area beyond the camp pitch black. The bandits wouldn't see him until it was too late.

But he had to hurry. They'd search the tents looking for valuables. When they discovered his HK rifle, they'd know they had more than they bargained for. They'd want to know who the rifle belonged to, and they might start shooting when nobody claimed the weapon.

Raven scooted across the ground on his belly.

Gray's voice: "What's the meaning of this?"

"I should be asking you!" the bandit leader snapped. He slapped Gray. He was a big man who filled his camouflage uniform. Hair cut close to his skull, no visible tattoos or other identifiable marks. Then again, Raven wasn't interested in identifying the man later.

He moved closer.

"You are in our territory without permission. Since you do not have permission, we will see what tribute you have available. If you have nothing we want, we'll take something anyway." And he leered at the young women. He grinned at the older women. "We will find something to make this violation of our space no worse than it has to be."

"We're missionaries," Gray shouted back. "We aren't here to hurt anybody."

"Oh? You are people of God? Which one?" The bandit leader laughed. "There are too many gods to keep track of. Do you know who *my* god is? No? He is me. *I am God.* And if you know what's good for you, you'll treat me with reverence."

Gray managed a nod. He looked along the line at the faces of his people. *At least they aren't shivering,* Raven decided. He moved a few more inches. Cold made panic worse, he'd learned. The hard way.

Another two inches forward. The spotlight still shined. The goons began tearing into the tents, and checking out the trucks.

Almost there.

Raven stopped a foot from the edge of the clearing. He had the line of sight he needed.

But he also had a rule.

No gunfights in public.

This wasn't public. The root of the rules was not to

endanger innocent people when a fight started. But he didn't have a choice this time. He had to take his chances.

He frowned. Did he?

Why not try another tactic?

Raven braced his pistol with both hands, lifted the muzzle, and prayed.

God, guide my bullets.

He eased back the trigger.

21

THE BANDIT LEADER WASN'T A BIG ENOUGH GOD. HE HAD NO power to stop the .45 bullet that punched through the side of his face and tore off his jaw.

As the shot cracked, the missionaries screamed. Gray screamed louder as blood spattered the front of his night shirt and the jawbone flew past his face. One of the medics with military experience kept his head, though. He shouted for everybody to get down, over and over, louder and louder. He led by example and shoved those nearest him into the dirt. The rest did likewise, getting out of the field of fire.

The remaining five bandits pivoted with their weapons, looking for who fired. They were still blind from the spotlight, which somebody shined into the forest. Raven shot out the light, then shot the man holding the light. He caught the next bandit high in the neck. He fell back into the buddy close to him, who managed to get a few shots off. His rifle rattled out a burst. The shots came nowhere near Raven. The Nighthawk Custom popped once more. Off went the top of the bandit's head.

Three remained. But instead of fighting, they took off running. The gunmen stomped into the forest.

Raven broke cover, jamming the hot .45 in the waistband of his jeans. The missionaries screamed as he emerged, but he ignored them. When they calmed down, their chatter quickly rose in volume. Raven grabbed the rifle of a fallen bandit and a spare mag. He told Gray to "check everybody" and took off running after the last three. Somebody yelled his name; a woman, probably Kaylee; he didn't respond. He had to stop the surviving gunmen from reaching home base. They'd bring back more troops to finish the fight.

Raven stayed low. He didn't need a bash in the head from a thick branch to end his fight before he stopped it on his own terms. He ran hard after the bandits, who didn't care how much noise they made—same as how they didn't care on their initial approach.

One of the gunners looked back and shouted an alarm. The gunners stopped short, almost losing balance as they spun around. A trio of gun muzzles swung Raven's way. He dived to the ground, going into a tuck-and-roll as the full-auto salvo sliced through the forest. He sprang up and returned fire, two shots; a shift of aim; two more. One of the gunners dropped. Raven flattened again and rolled left. More return fire. Somebody screamed as his weapon clicked empty and he hurried to reload. Raven stitched him stomach to neck with his own burst and the man tumbled clumsily into a tree to flop flat.

The last gunner decided to turn and run. But one of those low branches beaned him in the forehead. He staggered as he yelled. Raven's next burst cut off the yell and made it almost a short squeak. And when the gunner fell over, silence reclaimed the night.

Raven grunted in disgust. He rose and tossed the rifle on

the ground. Grabbing the pistol from his waistband, he walked back to the camp.

HE HEARD their excited voices before he returned. Gray tried to restore order. They'd set up lanterns to see by, but none were as bright as the spotlight. Raven noticed the shot-out light remained where it had fallen. So did the bodies.

The missionaries had changed from pajamas to street clothes. They were packing to leave and working fast.

Raven found Gray being tended to by his daughter and one of the missionaries who worked as a paramedic. He didn't look too bad, but pain from the blow to his belly still etched his face.

"Raven," Gray said. He stifled a wince as he spoke. "We owe you our lives."

"It's good you're packing to leave. I'd have suggested as much."

"We wouldn't have left without you."

"Assuming I came back."

"No, we knew you would. We prayed about it."

Another man asked Raven to help with the bodies. Some of the big guys were dragging the dead out of the camp and into the forest. A debate started about what to do with their weapons. Several men began helping themselves to either rifle or pistol, and ammunition. One told Raven he'd served two tours in Iraq; he knew how to handle a weapon. The others figured they'd be nice to have in case the bandits came back. Raven assured them the ones who'd attacked them would never bother anybody again. But he also appreciated the extra eyes who'd be watching out for retaliation same as he.

"All right, listen up!" Gray shouted. All eyes turned to

him. "We've had an unfortunate night, but praise God we're okay." Murmurs of agreement interrupted him. "But we need to get on the road and away from here in case anybody else comes along. I'm suggesting we head for Bogota and cut the trip short. Does anybody disagree?"

Nobody did, though two women expressed disappointment. They didn't think the group should abandon their last stop. Gray promised they'd come back and hit all the stops again, without fail. The two women were the only ones who wanted to stay and finish the mission. Raven understood. They'd come a long way and didn't want to go home thinking they'd failed. The others had had a scare and wanted to go home. Raven didn't blame them, either. Not everybody is cut out for dangerous environments, no matter their spiritual outlook.

In the end the majority ruled. The two women got their last shots in with a guilt trip about letting down the people they'd come to serve, but nobody was paying attention. The bandit attack had rattled many. Raven wanted to see what happened after they were a few miles from the camp site. It wouldn't surprise him if others started changing their tune, and wanted to finish what they'd come to do. Bandits or not.

But the decision didn't change, and the convoy rolled into Bogota a little after sunrise the next morning. The big church parking lot was empty, the building closed. The trucks and van parked anyway. Gray put in a call to the lead pastor and advised of their situation and early arrival. The fellow promised to come over and let them inside ASAP. In the meantime, everybody spread out to try and relax. The captured weapons remained covered in one of the trucks. Raven took the time to break down the HK and stow it in his backpack. He put his pistol in there, too. Then he sat with Gray and his daughter on a set of steps beside the building.

"Where do you go from here, Raven?" the doctor said.

"I'll get a hotel, and make some calls," Raven replied. "I need to let some people know what happened to my team."

"Look," Gray said, "I don't know where you came from, or where you're going. I know for sure where you're going is dangerous. We haven't known each other very long, but I know a good man when I see one. And you're a good man, Raven. God has a plan for you, whether you realize it or not. I hope wherever you go, you'll leave a door open for Him."

"I promise I will," Raven said. "I appreciate all of you and what you're doing." He addressed Kaylee. "Does cutting the mission short ruin your movie, Kaylee?"

"No," she said. She held tight to her father's left arm, leaning on his shoulder. "We'll be able to do the ending we want now that we're here."

"Good."

Nobody said much as the sun rose higher and warmed the streets. Then the pastor showed up and let the missionaries inside. Raven and Gray shook hands and said good-bye. Kaylee gave him a hug. Others wished Raven farewell, too. He gave them a last look. Kaylee's two friends, with their cameras, were filming; he didn't try to hide as the lens swept in his direction. They'd saved his life and he returned the favor. He wouldn't forget them anytime soon.

22

KENDRICK WARD STOOD ON THE PORCH OF HIS HOUSE. HE lived in the Historic District of Park Ridge, New Jersey. His home was his trophy, sitting atop a small hill overlooking the tree-lined street. Their sprawling branches and green leaves hung over the street like umbrellas. Great for blocking out the sun on hot days. More homes were set back from the road, each with immaculate green lawns. He was a king on this street, one of many. A king overseeing his part of the territory. His neighboring kings kept to themselves same as he did. The people who lived in the neighborhood enjoyed their privacy. They didn't want anything to disturb what they'd carved out for themselves.

Then the Lincoln sedan pulled into his driveway and stopped. Zac Fox exited the car and straightened his sport coat before coming forward. Ward *felt* like a king when he was going about his own business. In realty, he wasn't actually in charge of his current project. He was a peon. A servant to a bigger master. In reality, he knew Zac Fox exerted more control over Ward's life at the moment than he did. And the man for whom Zac Fox worked had ultimate control over both of their lives.

Fox climbed the stone steps and stepped onto the wood floor of the wrap-around porch. He was an imposing figure no matter how many times Ward met the man. Fox's beard remained thick and hearty and so did the rest of him. Ward extended a hand and they shook. But Ward noted Fox appeared troubled. Lips pressed together; brow furrowed; he asked that they go inside right away.

Ward noticed he held a tablet computer. He opened the door and led Fox inside.

More wood and stone made up the interior, with the kind of fancy furnishings only top dollar secured. The two men breezed through two rooms without stopping to admire anything. Ward gave his wife, in the kitchen, a hand signal meaning she wasn't to disturb them. He saw her nod of understanding.

Ward shut the door to his den. Fox approached the couch in the center of the room and sat. He told Ward to get a drink if he wanted; there was bad news to take in. He asked Ward to close the curtains. The den's wide windows made him nervous.

Ward didn't appreciate Fox giving orders in his own sanctuary. It only further cemented the fact he was a simple cog in a much larger machine. But now wasn't the time to argue. He shut the curtains but didn't fix a drink. He sat opposite Fox and asked for details.

Fox passed him the tablet. "Plenty of details in the pictures. Swipe left."

Ward did, but with a gasp. The grotesque photographs showed body parts, a portion of a forest in disarray. Bloody stumps and legs and torsos and heads that had once been men. Ward returned the tablet with a trembling hand. Now he needed a drink. He stood on shaky legs and found the corner bar. A few inches of whiskey in a glass went down rough, but then he returned to the couch.

"What happened?"

"What do you mean, what happened?" Fox said. "We took care of the mercenaries. Problem is, one's missing."

"Missing?"

"We got enough parts for five guys. Where's the sixth?"

"Oh, no."

"Yeah. Oh, no. Now, either the last man got vaporized, or he made it out and died elsewhere. Both of those options work to our advantage. The third option doesn't."

"What if he survived and comes after me?"

"Yup," Fox said.

"This is...this is..."

"A pile of shit."

"Yes! A big pile. What are we going to do?"

"We still have people in Colombia. They're trying to determine what parts belong to who. It's all we can do to see who was there and who got away."

"You're convinced the sixth man got away?"

"Me? Personally? Yes. But we won't know until we get some IDs and check around the area. We might get lucky and find the sixth guy a few yards away."

"How old is this information?" Ward asked.

"Couple hours. They're still on scene working."

"Okay. So it's not like—"

"No. These pictures weren't taken two days ago."

"Okay. All right. That's fine. We're learning and there's still time to learn more before we have to panic. Right. Okay." Ward's heavy breathing wouldn't stop. He felt like he'd run a marathon but he was sitting still. Don't panic? Hell, he was beyond panic.

"I guess," Ward said, "this was a chance we took."

"You finished your part of the job," Zac Fox said. "Wait for further orders. In the meantime, I'm taking care of this." He tapped the tablet. "Keep your head down and your mouth shut and we'll get to the end of this. Okay?"

"Fine, fine."

Fox rose to leave. Ward saw him out. He waved off his wife's questions from the kitchen as he returned to the den once more. He went behind his desk. His legs still shook and he sat down. Grabbing the phone, he dialed a long-distance number. Because he had a feeling who the sixth man was, and he knew the man hadn't died with the others. No way.

Ward had made one mistake trying to fill his mercenary team with the best.

He hired Sam Raven.

The phone rang in Ward's ear. He waited for an answer. The person who did pick up spoke Spanish, and Ward responded in kind. It wasn't until he gave a specific coded phrase that the person on the other end agreed to go and get the big boss. And he wasn't happy to hear Ward's voice. Ward pressed on. There were matters to discuss, and he wanted the top man's input. He knew better than to make any decisions the top man didn't agree with. He hadn't survived as a businessman in New York and New Jersey all these years by being an idiot.

23

CLARK WILSON ARRIVED FOR WORK AT THE CENTRAL Intelligence Agency at 8:45 am. The extra fifteen minutes allowed him to get coffee at the Starbucks in the commissary.

He arrived at the Special Activities Center. Nodding hello to the department receptionist, he proceeded into the bullpen. Analysts at desks sat in front of a trio of monitors. Each screen displayed data, usually a large amount of data. Their job was to sift through the information and present reports. Two stood near an electronic wall map discussing an area highlighted by a red dot. Two other managers, in their offices, looked like fish in an aquarium. Their desks sat behind glass walls. One could look in or out, but not hear what went on inside.

Entering his office behind a glass wall of his own, he set down the coffee and his briefcase. First order of business: check the alerts from overnight. As a Senior Staff Operations Officer, he was always one of the first to see mission updates. Messages requiring attention above his rank he forwarded to his boss.

He clicked on his email. Forty-eight messages had arrived in his inbox via field crews overnight. Wilson sipped his coffee and began reading through each one.

A message midway down the list made him put his coffee on his desk again. He read carefully. It wasn't a message from a field officer. The message was from the NSA, sent to his specific attention.

The email reported MAINSTAY had picked up a telephone conversation in which somebody mentioned flagged name.

MAINSTAY was the code name for the NSA "phone snooper" operation. The program monitored telephone conversations across the United States. The goal was to catch bad actors planning homeland attacks. Instead, to most of DC, it was a flagrant violation of privacy. Thanks to the Patriot Act, it was legal. Hey, Joe Public, say hello to your government masters the next time you use the phone. Or text. Or email. You want privacy in communications? Send smoke signals. Ain't no spy alive knows how to read those. And remember MAINSTAY is public knowledge; imagine what they're hiding. Also, none of this stopped 9/11. Sleep well, America.

Wilson read through to the end. Somebody in New Jersey named Kendrick Ward made an international all to an UNSUB (unknown subject). During the call, Ward said the name *Sam Raven.*

Wilson and Raven had a long history. They'd worked together at the CIA until Raven quit for a normal life. And Wilson was there when tragedy ripped away Raven's normal life and forced him back into the shadow world. He knew Raven lived on borrowed time, and submitted a request for the NSA to scan for mentions of Raven's name. He wanted to keep tabs on his often-absent friend. In case he ever needed a hand. Wilson had access to resources Raven lacked.

Wilson took a few minutes to research Kendrick Ward. He found more questions than answers. He also dug into the metadata of the phone conversation. He wanted to know the identity of the UNSUB.

He discovered Ward was a businessman in New Jersey with no official criminal record. But the DEA listed him as a person of interest in a case involving a Colombian cartel. They lacked solid proof of his involvement, however.

The UNSUB might have been his Colombian connection, but the metadata proved a dead end. The UNSUB had their end of the conversation redirected to several locations. NSA didn't have time to get a fix on the real origin of the call; Ward and UNSUB hadn't talked long enough.

Why would Ward, clean on the surface, have a talk with somebody who concealed his location via high-tech counter-measures?

The text of the conversation proved a few more clues, and only one conclusion.

"We made a mistake hiring him..."

"He might be dead with the others, have patience..."

"He'll come after me..."

Wherever he was, Raven had a target on his back.

Wilson needed to find him.

He tried the obvious first. He called Raven's cell phone.

THE SHOWER FELT GOOD. Raved washed the past couple of days away. His mind buzzed with next steps. Things he had to do. Like getting back to the United States to confront Kendrick Ward.

He dried off and pulled on a bathrobe.

He was in a room at the Bogota Marriott, on the top floor, with a view of the city. But he kept the curtains closed to keep a sniper from getting a shot at him. Paranoid, yes. There were people after him. Or would be, once they realized he survived the ambush.

After leaving the church, he waited for a bank to open. He wasn't entirely welcome. He smelled bad, his clothes were a mess, and the manager handled his business personally. Raven had his bank in Stockholm, where he lived, wire enough cash to get him a hotel room. And clothes. He asked a taxi driver for the nearest hotel, and the driver brought him to the Marriott. More strange looks at check-in. But they liked his money and didn't fuss. After spending a few quiet moments in his room, he went on a shopping trip to buy needed items. Back at the hotel, he finally showered and tried to force himself to relax. No dice.

But he tried. Stretched out on the bed, Raven let the quiet surround him. The hotel had solid walls and he heard very little from other guests in the hallway, or the rooms next door or above.

Most people, he noted from past observation, didn't like quiet. They needed noise to keep nervous thoughts from their minds. Thinking too much was uncomfortable. It was better to stay busy and distracted and not consider one's life too much. Raven was the opposite. He needed to think. He needed to acknowledge choices, good and bad, and consider the consequences of each. He tried not to think of what he might have done different to keep his team alive. The thoughts entered his mind anyway. And he had no solution, no "I should've done this, or that" to remove the guilt over surviving. He'd lived. His team hadn't. Dr. Gray thought he survived because God needed him. For what? Raven had lost so much, he often wondered what he had left to live for.

He kept his past in the sterling silver locket he wore around his neck. His past was always with him, guiding him, directing him from one dangerous encounter to the next. But in those encounters he often championed those who had no power of their own. Or not enough power. He saved lives. Sometimes people died despite his efforts, and he had to live with those losses, too. It wasn't much of a life, but it was the one chosen for him. He had no way to break away. Despite his desire to find peace, he knew he couldn't abandon his war without end. Too many innocent people would suffer if he gave up, so he pressed on.

There had been times, off and on, when it appeared he found a respite, the peace he so desired. Then he lost it again. Like Sisyphus, he was condemned to reach the top of the mountain only to fall back to the bottom again.

In the end he had no idea what he could have done differently. Sometimes you did everything right and still got killed. It was a fact of life. Whoever ambushed them knew where to find them. Obviously, Ward played a role. But how big a part? He needed to find out. He needed to settle the score.

His cell rang.

24

RAVEN ROLLED OFF THE BED AND SORTED THROUGH THE PILE of clothes on the floor beside the bed. He found his cell phone in the pocket of his old jeans. The ringtone identified the caller. He knew it was Clark Wilson at the CIA. He answered.

"Clark," Raven said.

"You've alive." Statement, not a question.

"Barely. What do you know?"

"NSA picked up a phone call between New Jersey and Colombia and your name came up." Wilson explained more about the report, and asked: "Who is Kendrick Ward?"

Now it was Raven's turn. He supplied details of his side of the story. He began with the meeting in New Jersey and concluding with the ambush. But he had a question of his own. "How did my connection not pick up the DEA's interest in Ward?"

Wilson laughed. "Your connection doesn't run deep enough. In this case, anyway. The DEA file is need-to-know."

"Some good men died here, Clark. I'm going to get to the bottom of this."

"Were there any signs this operation wasn't what you thought?"

The question hit hard. Yeah, Raven thought to himself. He told Clark about the misgivings brought up by Fireplug Starkey. The presence of Zac Fox, the former mafia torpedo. The doubts raised by Pope.

"But I talked to Ward in front of everybody," Raven said, "and he more or less answered the questions. I didn't see them as red flags after we talked."

"Don't go in circles about it."

"You weren't there, Clark."

"And I know you, too. You're going to spin yourself into a tizzy. It happened. You can't change it."

Raven wanted to put the conversation back where he was comfortable. Talking about action.

"Any chance I can talk to the agents involved? I mean the people on the Bogota end. I can tell them what happened and we can help each other."

"They won't like you moving on their territory," Wilson said. "Anybody who knows you knows full well what you intend to do."

"I'd rather they see I'm here rather than have an accident later. It would be a shame to shoot a DEA guy by mistake."

"I'll make a few calls. You going to hang around a bit?"

"I will stay put in my hotel room till I hear from you."

"Won't be long," Wilson said.

They ended the call. Raven paced the room. There wasn't much space to pace. The area between the foot of the bed and the wall-mounted television was only a few feet. He'd selected a regular room rather than a suite. He didn't need the extra space. All he needed was a bed and a shower. *Far more than my team got...*

Stop the guilt trip. There was nothing you could have done and had things turned out differently those rockets would have killed you, too.

He stopped and let out a frustrated breath at the closed curtains. He turned and stretched out on the bed again.

More questions. Ward and the DEA. Who was the UNSUB?

Ward had managed to fool him. Big time. He had a great sob story playing to Raven's weakness. He'd used his dead daughter as a plot. The move didn't make sense. How could a father do that?

Yeah, Ward had fooled him.

Raven did not intend to let anyone fool him again.

He'd find out who was responsible, and why, and show them the meaning of *payback*.

THE NEXT MORNING, Raven followed directions. He took a walk along Avenida Carrera 7. Wilson had called back the previous evening, told Raven the DEA agreed to see him, and to take a walk. They'd find *him*. Wilson also advised he travel unarmed, but Raven wasn't about to go naked. He wore the Nighthawk .45 under his left arm in the speed rig, as usual. A windbreak covered the shoulder harness.

The Avenida looked like any other road in the word. Two lanes going opposite directions, an island down the middle. A long line of tall trees grew from the island and shaded each side of the road. Motorists, bicyclists, pedestrians—normal lives. Raven walked among them with his abnormal life and nobody knew the difference. But he did. He knew he didn't belong with them.

He walked in the shadows of the trees. Passed shops and restaurants. He heard English mixed with the native language, spoken by white Europeans. Odd to see, but evidence of a world growing smaller and smaller. Nobody paid him any attention. He was simply another body on the street.

He kept walking.

What did the DEA have in mind? A street pick-up? He tried not to think about it as he approached a corner. Calle 76, according to the map he consulted on his phone. He pocketed the cell. As he turned the corner, more trees shaded him from the sun, and a black van screeched to a stop at the curb.

The driver overshot; the front driver's side tire bumped up the curb. Raven recoiled as the side door open and two people in black, wearing ski masks, grabbed him. One of the figures was slight but male; the other had tits and small hands. He let them haul him into the van. The side door slammed shut. The van jolted up and down as the tire left the curb. The driver steered back into the street and stepped on the accelerator.

Raven grunted as he sat up. They'd removed the middle seats. The carpeting beneath him was thin and scratchy. He scooted against the passenger side wall, but its curvature hurt his back. He scooted forward and with his hands on the carpet behind him.

"A little rude, don't you think?" he said.

The two figures removed their ski masks. The woman's hair spilled down her back.

"I'm Hollie Chandler, DEA Supervisor," she said. "This is my associate, Brad Patel."

"Hi," Patel said. He extended a hand. Raven shook. Hollie did not offer hers.

"Why the carnival act?" Raven said. "How many witnesses saw that?"

"Zero," Hollie said. "You can bet all eyes turned away when we showed up. It's such a common sight, nobody bothers. It's much better than meeting at a place where we'll have eyes on us the entire time."

"The cartels have spies everywhere?"

"There's nowhere they *don't* have somebody watching," she said.

"Fair enough," Raven said. "Do we talk here or what?"

"We can make you more comfortable, sure," Hollie said. "It'll take a few minutes to get there."

Raven hoped it wasn't a long wait.

"You can keep your gun," Hollie said.

"Gee, thanks," Raven told her.

"Give her some credit," Patel announced. "She thought we'd be able to take it from you. I told her no way."

"Did you put any money on it?"

He grinned. "Who'd have won?"

Raven didn't smile. "You."

Patel turned to Hollie and let out loud, "Ha!" He added, "Told you."

Hollie shook her head.

Twenty minutes later, the van rolled through the gate of a gray concrete building. Raven noticed the wire mesh covering each window. No discernible identification signs. Neither DEA agent offered to tell him where they were.

They escorted him down a cold concrete hallway with flickering fluorescent lights above. Through a heavy door into a small room with a table and chairs.

"Interrogation room?" Raven said.

Patel pushed the door shut. "For your safety."

"And ours," Hollie said. "This keeps you out of sight of the people upstairs."

Raven folded his arms. "How bad are the leaks?"

"So far, so good," Patel told him. "We're only being careful."

"We've vetted every man working on our task force backwards and forwards," Hollie said. "We don't have any traitors here."

"Yet," Raven added.

"What Patel said then," she offered. "Want to sit down?"

Raven laughed. "And feel like a prisoner? All we're missing is the handcuffs."

Hollie took one of the chairs. Patel joined her. The chairs were metal, and their legs scraped on the concrete floor. The chill in the room made Raven glad for the windbreaker.

The DEA agents looked at Raven and waited. He finally sat across from them and put his arms on the table.

"All right," he said. "Let's compare notes."

"You have the more interesting story," Hollie told him. "Care to start? We'll fill in what we can."

Raven told his story again and left nothing out. Hollie and Patel listened without interruption. When Raven stopped, Hollie spoke first.

"Well, Ward wasn't lying about the daughter."

"But he sure as hell twisted the story," Patel added.

"How?"

"By claiming Sevilla was responsible," Patel said. "There was no way he could know. Unless he squeezed enough street pushers to get to the top and find the connection that way. And I doubt he has the skills."

"What about Zac Fox? Would he be able to find the source?"

"It doesn't matter," Hollie said. "You're chasing a rabbit. Ward had a reason for getting rid of Sevilla, and he told you a story to make it sound good."

"Please explain," Raven said.

"As you know, we're investigating Ward," Hollie said. "He has a friend in Colombia named Antonio Panadero. Panadero wants to control the East Coast of the United States. He wants to be the sole provider of cocaine, heroin, pills, etcetera. Sevilla already runs the East Coast distribution network. Sevilla was in the way."

Raven frowned. "But getting rid of Sevilla won't open the territory. Whoever takes over—"

"Never mind whoever takes over," the woman said. "Sevilla has a daughter, whom you saw on the video. She'll want to know who killed her father. She'll want the same thing you do, but for a different reason."

"Then why would Panadero kill Sevilla?"

"Because the mob families on the East Coast," she said, "depend on a steady drug supply. They will *not* appreciate the gap in product. Panadero will be able to step in because he has stuff to sell while Sevilla's survivors are tripping over their dicks to find out who's taking over. In other words, it's going to be a while before Sevilla's daughter can do anything about Panadero. He'll take over the East Coast supply line while *she* fights to survive. And once she finally takes over her father's organization, she can get her revenge."

"What is Ward's part of the job?" Raven asked.

"He knows *certain people* through his work," Hollie said. "All the mobsters he has to make nice with? The ones he hired Zac Fox to help him talk to? He can arrange the meetings Panadero needs. He's the go-between."

"But you can't prove it," Raven said.

"About all we can prove right now," Patel offered, "is what Ward had for breakfast this morning."

Raven opened his mouth to say more, but Hollie Chandler cut him off.

"Now, Mr. Raven, you need to listen. We can't have you messing around in our investigation. We know your reputation, you've been a help in the past, we understand why you're upset, but this time we need to ask you to stand down. Let us do our job."

Raven didn't reply.

"All right, I'll make it simple," she said. *"Back off."*

Raven raised an eyebrow and folded his arms.

25

"ARE YOU LISTENING TO ME?" HOLLIE WANTED TO KNOW.

Raven glanced at Patel. The room felt colder now. The DEA pair weren't friends; they were sharks looking for a meal.

Raven corrected himself. They never *were* his friends.

"We're in agreement, Mr. Raven," the other man said. He cleared his throat and shifted in his seat. Confrontation wasn't his thing. "With all due respect for what you went through, you need to stay out of this."

"How close are you?" Raven said. "To closing down this alliance, I mean."

"Close enough," Patel continued.

"Be careful, Brad," Hollie said.

"No, he deserves to know." Before she argued further, Patel continued. "We're targeting Panadero's accountant. He knows everything. We want to turn him to our side. We want *him* bring us the books. He can tell us where the money goes, who gets it, everything possible to freeze Panadero's finances and bring him down."

"I suppose," Raven said, "you know for sure he'll flip?"

"He has wants and needs we can appeal to," Patel said. "We'll give him assurance he can get out of Colombia in one piece with a clean slate."

"What's on the slate?"

"Embezzlement. Panadero hangs the threat of prosecution over the accountant to keep him in line."

Raven knew better than to ask the man's name. They were willing to share, but the accountant's name would be too much. He didn't put much faith in the flip, anyway. How much would the accountant really know? Men like Panadero knew how to cover their tracks. They knew how to make sure no single person ever knew all there was to know about the business.

But Raven knew another truth. Once you take down one brick, the others follow. The accountant was the first brick.

They wanted him to walk away when he had five good reasons to stay. But the DEA pair made an honest appeal and he understood. To go charging in like a bull would ruin thousands of work hours. They wanted the cartels stopped as much as he did. And like he told Ward, removing one narco from the equation wouldn't stem the narcotic tide.

But...

Raven was out for revenge. Stopping the drug flow wasn't on his mind. At all. He wanted to kill the people who'd set him up. And murdered five good men in the process.

He kept his arms folded and thought it over. If the enemy believed he was dead, they'd continue the plan. By continuing, they'd expose vulnerabilities. He knew about the plan now; there were other ways to interdict without running the DEA's setup. And if Ward and Panadero didn't believe he was dead, he had an idea on how to exploit their fear of his return.

"I could be a jerk and demand a favor in return for walking away," Raven said, "but I see no value there."

"You'll have your hands full," Hollie said, "staying alive once Yasmina Sevilla learns you killed her old man."

"Is that a threat?"

"We'll say, for purposes of our discussion, there's a target on your back already."

"Always is, sweetie."

A red flush crept up her neck. She looked mad.

"Okay, I'm out. For now."

"For *good*," Hollie said.

Raven shook his head. "We both know you'll need me. I'll be waiting."

"It'll be a long wait," she said.

"I have plenty of time," Raven told her. "You got a plan to get me back to my hotel?"

"We'll give you a ride" Patel told him.

Fair enough, Raven decided.

BACK AT THE HOTEL, Raven updated Wilson. The CIA man promised to get Raven a seat on a CIA plane leaving Bogota the next morning.

Raven met the flight crew and three other passengers in a private hanger. Nobody gave their names. They accepted Raven aboard after he provided a coded phrase Wilson gave him. He sat in the back of the jet. The other three passengers took seats up front. It was a quiet flight.

Wilson met him at Dulles and they climbed into Wilson's car. Raven's temporary diplomatic immunity status helped him by pass customs. His passport wasn't exactly in order.

Wilson drove him away from the airport.

"Nice flight?" Wilson said.

"Thanks for the ride. I have a lot of my mind and it was good to sit and think."

"About what?"

"Ward, for one. He played his roll well. Had me fooled. There was a moment when we first met where I thought we had a thing or two in common. We don't. Never did."

"His daughter *did* die, Sam."

"But he exploited her. For some reason. I'm going to find out."

"You're going to ignore the DEA?" Wilson said.

"They know how to make somebody disappear as well as me, Clark. What would you have done?"

Wilson drove on.

RAVEN FOUND another hotel and agreed to wait for Clark.

"I can't cater to the demands of Sam Raven," he said. "I have a job, you know."

But Wilson showed up around dinner time. He told Raven the food was on him. They ordered from room service. Raven stood behind Wilson as the CIA man booted up a laptop on the corner desk.

"Panadero has a lot on his plate," Wilson said. He accessed a file. "Not only cartel business, but he's in the middle of a romantic triangle in his own home."

Raven was intrigued.

"He's blissfully unaware," Wilson added. "His wife has been having an affair with his number two for decades. In fact, the second-in-command is really the father of Panadero's daughter."

"Interesting," Raven said. "Why is he ignorant?"

"Too busy chasing any skirt younger than his wife," Wilson said.

Wilson gave Raven a rundown of Panadero's associates, assorted gunmen and hangers-on. He showed Raven their dossiers, too. The CIA had all the data required. They knew Panadero inside and out. Yet the narcos roamed freely. As if their existence benefited US law enforcement and certain politicians in particular. Corruption was the name of the game. They weren't necessarily taking narco pay-offs. But the fact was, fighting a drug war cost millions of dollars. Some of those millions found their way into the pockets of the most ardent drug war hawks. If the cartels were wiped out, the gravy train stopped. They took down one now and then to show progress in "the war", but the fight continued. Cartels merged, leaders replaced, the flow of narcotics never stopped.

When dinner arrived, Wilson closed down the laptop. He and Raven found other topics to discuss while they ate.

———

RAVEN TOOK a walk after Wilson departed. He felt good about their meeting; it felt good to be alive, too. Alive to go back and finish what another had started. To settle a score.

He turned left on Main Ave after exiting the hotel, and headed for the intersection at 14th Street ahead. He paused there. Traffic went by; a few other pedestrians, too. The people passing him were locals, he figured. The Jefferson Memorial, lit brightly, sat opposite the intersection in the Tidal Basin. None of them stopped to admire the structure. The columns and domes and the shadow of the Jefferson statue reminded Raven of something he'd learned long ago. People were made for great things. But they often settled for far less than they were capable of. Grand adventures or hair-raising risks weren't required. All one needed to be was their best in the time in which they lived. Small scale, large scale, it didn't matter. Human beings were made for more than staring at television screens or wasting their lives in a thought stream of what-ifs and wouldn't-it-be-nice. Humans were called to do, not sit. But called by whom? The Universe? The God of the missionaries in Colombia? As Raven reflected on the image beyond, he understood his own purpose a little more. Understood why people like Dr. Gray and his daughter Kaylee did what they did, despite the risks. Because they had to. Could he do any less?

He turned away from the memorial and walked up 14th toward Independence Avenue. He'd pass the Holocaust Museum along the way. The Jefferson Memorial and the museum book-ended each other. One representing the horror of man, the other representing the will to stand up to such horror. Raven hadn't planned to stay in DC, but the ghosts of battles past had other plans. They put him where he needed to be. They wanted him to remember why he existed, and why the war without end was important. Somebody had to stand up to the horrors of man. Raven had been selected, like many others. He might never cross paths with the others, but he knew they were out there. Brothers and sisters at arms who'd die to stop Animal Man.

Raven's thoughts stopped. He wasn't alone on the sidewalk.

A glance back. Two men. One wearing a black jacket, the other a long coat and skull cap. Alarm bells sounded in his head. They weren't locals; they kept their distance. He was being followed.

The cartel? No.

The DEA.

Chandler and Patel didn't trust him. They'd put him under surveillance to make sure he didn't go charging back to Colombia to raise hell.

Well.

So be it.

Now wasn't the time to fight. But he had plans. He'd have

to shake the watchers later. Violence was out of the question. He wasn't going to beat the garbage out of people on the same side. They were only following orders. They'd have been told to only watch him and report back. Nothing else. If they knew the whole story, they might even look the other way as Raven slipped out of the hotel one last time. It was enough to know they were there. The knowledge would keep him from getting sloppy.

Tonight, all he wanted was a walk. Try to relax. Clear his head with fresh air. He'd go a few blocks, take the watchers with him, and get an idea of their style and approach. Then he'd file the information away. For next time.

He kept walking.

26

ANTONIO PANADERO NEVER HAD TROUBLE ATTRACTING FEMALE attention. Even at 50, he was still trim, still had his hair, and exuded bad boy confidence.

He employed some of that confidence as he hustled across a busy street. He had his eye on an apartment building a block away, and a ravishing beauty in one of those apartments. But he had to give the DEA agents watching him a run for their money first.

They were always in the background. Always watching. They never did anything but watch. Surely, they mapped his movements, and he wasn't one to vary too much from routine. He liked a woman every week. Every Wednesday, to be precise. But what did knowing his routine give them? Nothing. What did it give him? A chance to say he wasn't bothered by them without having to say he wasn't bothered by them. To flaunt his continued freedom in their faces. To remind them they had no real power over him or any other cartel boss.

He reached the sidewalk and continued. The agents wouldn't run across the street to keep up. By now, they knew where he was going and with whom he planned to spend an hour or two. Agents at the headquarters would make appropriate notations in the log book. And they'd play hide and seek again another day.

Panadero didn't use his bodyguards on these sojourns. He didn't want anybody listening to him and his lady friend doing the deed. A guy had to have some privacy, after all. Especially if things got rough. They often did.

He reached the apartment building and entered the lobby. A quick elevator ride took him to the 10th floor. He didn't have bodyguards, but he wasn't unarmed. A Glock 9mm rode under his jacket. He wasn't a baby who couldn't feed itself. He knew how to handle the weapon and worked to keep his shooting eye sharp. If the need ever arose, if he was every called upon to make a last stand, he intended to do so with a gun in his hand. And *not* by hiding behind a bodyguard. A man had to have standards, too.

Apartment 1045. He knocked on the door, a coded tap worked out over the years. When the door opened, *she* stood back to let him inside.

She was Sandra Hurtado. Total MILF if there ever was one, but you'd never know she'd spit out a kid by looking at her. Curves for days, big round breasts, long dark hair, smoldering dark eyes. Her curves were barely concealed by the low-cut nightie she wore—at four o'clock in the afternoon. No bottoms, as usual. As *commanded* by Panadero. But she looked nervous as he entered. She shut the door fast.

"What's wrong?" he asked.

"What do you mean?" she said. "I'm in the doorway with my lady its exposed!"

He smiled and pulled her to him. She winced when she felt the butt of the Glock dig into her.

"Those lady bits belong to *me*, my dear."

"Do you ever listen to yourself?"

She tilted her head back and tried not to grimace as he kissed her neck and nibbled an earlobe. Then she melted a little as the tingles ran through her body. Yeah, he was a brute. But dammit he knew how to operate the equipment.

He scooped her off her feet and carried her into the plush living room full of furniture he'd provided. Or his money provided, rather. He dropped her on the couch, where she stretched out and spread her legs. She licked her lips in anticipation and invitation and he got out of his clothes in a hurry. The shoulder harness containing the Glock he placed on the glass coffee table.

He was on her and in her before she knew it, but the surprise didn't last long. *Every* woman in his stable knew when Panadero parted the pink curtains. Soon his thrusting became all she thought about as she wrapped arms and legs around him and urged him on...

They switched positions for the second round. He sat back on the couch, climbed onto his lap, and he slipped inside again. And he filled his hands with her curves. He fondled and caressed every inch of her smooth skin. She rode him up the mountain again and they both tumbled down together...

Afterwards, he sat smoking a cigarette while she curled up beside him. She didn't worry about the wet spots on the couch. They cleaned up easily enough.

"Can we skip next Wednesday? Or move to another day?" she said.

"No." He blew a smoke ring.

"But my daughter—"

"Hell with your daughter. I pay you. I pay for *this*." He gestured angrily around the room. "You do what I say *when* I say it, and I say Wednesday."

She went quiet.

"Did I hear *you* say *okay*, Sandra?"

"I'll find somebody else to take her."

"Good."

"But why can't you—"

He shoved her away from him. As the cigarette dangled in his mouth, he grabbed her by the neck and squeezed. Sandra's smoldering dark eyes went wide, filled with fear, and she let out choked cries of protest.

"You *know* me," he said, leaning on her. "You know *better* than to keep asking after I've told you no."

She didn't try to fight him off. She submitted and her eyes pleaded with him to stop. When he let go, she gasped for air, hand to her heart, turning away from him. But she didn't leave the couch.

Panadero got up in disgust. He dressed again as she sobbed.

"Same time next week," he told her, and made his exit.

27

PANADERO FOUND THE LIMOUSINE WAITING FOR HIM AT THE curb. He hopped in the back seat. Another man already sat inside. The man gave Panadero a disapproving glance.

"Something on your mind, Salvador?"

Salvador Costa was Panadero's second-in-command. One of the few men Panadero trusted. They'd grown up on the streets together. Panadero was the leader; Sal Costa the detail man.

"These antics of yours, Tony—"

"Are my business." He yelled for the driver to go. The driver put the car in gear and joined the flow of traffic. Panadero pressed a button and a plastic partition between the back and front rose, blocking them off from the driver. He didn't want his people privy to his private conversation, especially a driver, who held such a low rank.

"What if one of your girlfriends ever stabs you to death?"

"They can try." He smirked. He watched the passing scenery.

Costa said nothing more for a few moments. The tinted

windows kept the bright light outside at bay. Then: "We have to talk about the latest."

"Tell me the latest, Sal. I'm listening."

"Sevilla's organization is in disarray, as we predicted."

"As *I* predicted."

"The result wasn't a stretch of the imagination in any way, Tony. Come on. We all knew a power struggle would result. We counted on it."

"Who's winning?"

"As of now, nobody. But the bodies are stacking up. Yasmina, Sevilla's daughter, is rallying those loyal to her father. She will emerge victorious, but not for a while. There's plenty of others who will try for the big chair."

"Good. Keep them too busy to worry about us. We'll slip into their US territory like a knife through butter." He laughed. "Or should I say—"

"Don't," Costa said.

Panadero laughed again.

"Then there's Ward," Costa said.

"Is he still acting like a little girl? Jumping at shadows?" Panadero asked. "You should have heard my last conversation with him, Sal. He acts as if the boogey man is coming for him."

"He's made no more remarks to me about the Raven fellow," Costa said. "He's making his appointments. Things are progressing. Slowly."

"Too slow."

"We can't rush, Tony."

"I know we can't rush, Sal. But I wish we could move *faster.*"

"And what about Raven? Can we really not consider him a threat?"

"Any sign of a body?"

"No body, and no live sightings, either."

"Then he's dead," Panadero stated.

"I'm not so sure."

"You agree with Ward?"

"I agree we don't have the concrete solution we need."

"There was a risk in hiring the mercenaries," Panadero said. "We're facing the risk—one or more surviving. But what can one man do against us?"

"Raven is more than one man."

Panadero laughed again. "He's a *tool*. A sharp tool. I wanted him for a reason. He was the best man to lead the team, somebody who lent legitimacy to the effort. And he did his job to perfection."

"He'll destroy everything you've worked for."

"What are you saying?" Panadero twisted in the seat to scowl at his number two. "We are more powerful than *one man* might ever achieve. I don't care what kind of army he raises."

"We have to remain vigilant."

"All right. We will remain vigilant. Make sure the lookouts keep looking. Provide them with incentives so they don't get bored. I want all eyes watching for Raven *just in case* he's still alive."

"Do we focus on Bogota or the US, too?"

"Bogota is fine. If he made it back to the US, we don't have to worry till he shows up here again."

Costa turned to look out the window.

"Anything else, Sal?"

"Not right now."

They continued the ride in silence.

But a fuse burned inside Panadero's mind. He knew Costa wanted to say more. But his friend also knew when to hold his tongue. Right now, he held his tongue.

IT WAS A HARD LIFE.

But Salvador Costa knew he wasn't taking an easy path when he joined and Antonio Panadero. Friends first, and later associates. They had clawed to the top of the cartel food chain together, kicking, fighting, killing. Now the prize belonged to them, but at a cost.

A great cost. They were men forever looking over their shoulders for the next threat.

He wandered the wrap-around walkway on the second level of the Panadero mansion. The big house sat in the middle of the sprawling estate. Green grass, gardens, two swimming pools and a pair of tennis courts surrounded the home.

It was hot. It was always hot and he no longer paid attention to the temperature. He walked with his hands clasped behind his back and gazed at the mountains in the distance.

He'd been taking risks his entire life and gambling on the outcome. So far, he'd been lucky—he was still alive. And no risk was greater than the night he and Marina Panadero began their relationship.

The affair wasn't one either planned. But the two wound up drawn together as they dealt with the extremes of Antonio's personality. One thing led to another, and another, and then Marina became pregnant. With *his* child. But she had to convince her husband the baby belonged to him—which wasn't difficult. Salvador Costa was forced to watch from the outside. While another man raised his daughter. While he and Marina exchanged glances full of meaning but said nothing out loud.

For a man who walked a tightrope between life and death every day, Salvador Costa played his part well. He was the friend / advisor to a powerful man. Panadero had a very short list of people he trusted. Costa was at the top of the list. His wife was second on the list. Sometimes, Costa knew, she dropped to third place. But Costa never fell from the pole position.

He paused to watch the landscaping crew tend the grass. Another crew cleaned the tennis court, making sure the play area remained spotless. Panadero was a passionate tennis player, and Costa his usual challenger. They played well together. The games were a chance to work out frustrations, let their minds focus on something other than work. Costa won as often as he lost; neither kept track of who won more. It wasn't the point of the game.

Light piano music drifted through the air. Costa smiled and quickened his step. He re-entered the house through a side door and found his way to the library. Sitting at the piano, playing with practiced ease, was Triana. His daughter.

He watched from the doorway. She had her eyes on the music sheet and didn't know he was there. Triana was a spitting image of her mother at 24, the same slight build, same mane of black hair. Triana wore a flower-print dress with her hair tied back. Her slender fingers flew over the keys as if she'd been born to play, and perhaps she had.

A second women entered from the opposite side of the room. Marina. Triana's mother. The older woman had lost none of her charm or beauty in the last 24 years, though she was a little thicker now. On her, it looked good. She stopped at the piano to watch her daughter play, then noticed Costa in the doorway. Their eyes met. She smiled. He smiled. It was a smile of pride, but hurt lingered behind his eyes. He had to remain distant. There was no other choice, if they wanted to live. And Costa had every intention of living long enough to see Triana become the woman God intended her to be.

He didn't hold onto the ridiculous hope that one day the truth would come to light and they'd live happily ever after. Panadero was a target of the Colombian government and the United States. Sooner or later, they'd fall to the relentless pursuit of law enforcement. And if Panadero ever learned the truth, they'd fall to the bullets from his gun.

Costa would take the secret to his grave.

But in moments like this, he could dream. He listened to his daughter play. She had a concert coming up, at the prestigious León de Greiff Auditorium, and they'd all go into the city to watch. He looked forward to the evening. A bright spot in an otherwise painful existence.

28

TRIANA PANADERO STOPPED PLAYING AND LOOKED AT HER mother. "What do you think?"

"Is this the composition you and Omar wrote?"

Triana nodded. "We'll perform it tomorrow. But it's missing something."

"What?"

"I don't know. And that's what bothers me. How do I know it's any good if I think something isn't right?"

Her mother glanced over her shoulder. "Why don't you ask your unofficial audience?"

Triana turned. She smiled. "What did you think, Uncle Sal?"

Costa remained in the doorway. "It's beautiful as-is, just like the woman who composed it."

She blushed and faced the keys again. She played a few random notes. She wasn't used to praise. She expected everybody to be indifferent or hostile. She didn't know why. Other artists and performers wrote about doubting work the public loved. Maybe, she decided, she really was one of them. Her reactions were a natural outgrowth of the creative process.

There was always something missing. Always something to fix. And all those thoughts came from the artist's own insecurities. But while she understood the thoughts in her head, her heart didn't take heed. Deep down she still thought she could improve composition. But it would never be perfect.

"I guess we'll see tomorrow," she said. She stopped playing and addressed her mother again. "Should we do the final alterations on my dress now?"

"After lunch. Which is ready, by the way." To Costa, her mother said: "Will you join us, Sal?"

Costa said no. He had other work to do. He left the doorway with the promise to see them later.

Triana tapped keys again. She didn't notice her mother staring at the now-empty doorway.

TRIANA WAS part of a youth orchestra, though at eighteen years of age, she was about to age out of the group. But not till after the concert at the León de Greiff Auditorium. The group planned to play the usual classical favorites along with original work.

Antonio Panadero did not like wearing tuxedos, but he made the exception for Triana's performance. And, of course, he arranged for the best seats in the house. In this case, an upper-level box where he, Marina, and Costa had privacy. They also had a full view of the stage and the general audience. The door behind them was locked with a guard posted. A guard Panadero trusted.

The domed roof and acoustical tiles made the orchestra sounds swell, and fill the space. The walls shook with musical vibrations. Each section of the thirty-piece orchestra, from brass to find and everything in between, sounded much larger than they were. Antonio Panadero sat and watched with a giant grin across his face. He almost forgot his wife and close confidant were on either side. He finally turned to Marina when Triana's number began. Their daughter sat at the piano and began the soft opening, the audience quiet. The high notes echoed like wind-chimes, with a haunting melody, something tragic. Then her volume and tempo increased. When Omar, her bandmate and co-writer, contributed a mournful violin accompaniment, he completed the picture. The pair fell in sync right away. They produced music with so much power and emotion within the notes that when the last note faded, the audience only had one reaction. They cheered and stood to applaud.

Panadero stood. He looked down on Triana as if a god from Olympus. She was the best of him. Her art would carry her away from the life he led, into a world where he might never be welcome, but she'd be safe. All he wanted was for her to be safe. His criminal activity began as a need to survive growing up on the streets. He'd come from a poor family with limited options. Faced with few choices, Panadero took the easiest option available. He didn't want the same for his daughter. She'd have better chances; a better life; and she had it at her doorstep after tonight. He didn't know what her next move would be after she departed the youth orchestra. Based on the standing ovation, he knew she'd find the right path. And if he only watched from the sidelines, he'd feel satisfied; he'd done his fatherly duty. Because of him, she'd beaten the odds. She'd never gone hungry. She hadn't needed to find ways to survive that took something from her soul, as it had his. It was too late for him to change; plus, he liked the power. It was intoxicating. More powerful than the drugs he peddled to users all over the world. But he'd saved Triana from such a potent cocktail. If he'd done nothing else right in his life, he did right by her.

Tonight, he experienced a different kind of power, the

power generated by Triana's passionate performance. She'd come a long way from the little girl fascinated by the sounds of the family piano. Investing in her natural talent was one of the wisest things he'd done.

Suddenly remembering his wife, he pulled her close for a squeeze. Costa was all smiles, too. "Uncle Sal," she called him. He'd been a constant in Triana's life same as he had Panadero's. The cartel leader considered Sal every much his equal. He couldn't run the business without Sal's guiding hands and advice. Sal gave Panadero a pat on the back. Panadero disengaged from his wife to shake his friend's hand.

The applause died down and the audience resumed their seats. Triana and Omar returned to their spots in the orchestra, and the show continued. Panadero was still basking in the glow. But the previous act was hard to follow, and the selection from Beethoven they played seemed dry.

───────────

WITH ANTONIO BETWEEN THEM, Sal and Marina only managed a few smiling glances at one another. But considering how Antonio behaved as if his wife wasn't there, Sal could have moved to her side for more. But doing so would have been hard to explain when Antonio finally remembered he wasn't alone. Stupid fool. If only he hadn't let money and power go to his head, Triana might be his daughter for real.

He watched as the performance resumed. The boss stared down with wide eyes. He was the only one in the box, as far as he was concerned. One thing Sal never understood was Antonio's selfishness. Except to the girl he believed was his daughter.

If the truth ever came out...

Salvador Costa didn't want to think about the consequences.

He thought about them often enough already.

JUST ONCE, Marina Panadero thought, it would be nice to celebrate with Triana's real father.

She settled in her seat once the performance began again. The rich music filled the hall. If she was light enough, the sounds could carry her away from the duplicity and secrets she lived with.

She'd known was she was getting into when she married Antonio. Her mother told her. And her mother knew firsthand. She married another type of Antonio Panadero. Her mother told her he'd treat her like staff. Expect the affairs, the mistresses. Expect to have access to money, but never forget who the money belonged to. And expect her new husband to use money to control her.

But her mother had not told her to look out for a man she would love more than the man she married. Her mother never told her how to pretend it wasn't true, especially after their child was born.

Eighteen years. She'd kept the secret for eighteen years. It was second-nature now. The deception, the careful peeks over her shoulder when she and Sal had a few seconds between them. Eighteen years. And part of her enjoyed making a fool of Antonio, because most days the son of a bitch deserved to know he was cucked...

But tonight was for Triana. She let the music carry her away.

29

BACKSTAGE AFTER THE CONCERT. A MADHOUSE OF NOISE. Sheer pandemonium as excited musicians reacted to the applause of the audience. They congratulated each other, high fives and kisses. Some dried tears of joy. Others hurried into private dressing rooms to get out of formal clothes and into outfits for the after party.

Triana made the rounds to her orchestra mates, then sneaked into a changing room. Her slinky black dress with the sparkly sequins fit her well, but she made no effort to remove it. She instead stood beside the door, near the hinges, and waited for it to open again.

Her performance with Omar had gone better than expected. Nobody disliked what they wrote. But sections of the music still seemed hollow and her wondered how to make it better. She was trying to think of a new arrangement altogether when the door opened halfway. Omar Acin stepped inside, shut the door, and almost lost his balance as Triana threw herself at him.

They laughed as they embraced, and then kissed long and

hard. He was as tall as her and almost as thin. She started removing his tux but he stopped her.

"Now?"

"It's perfect," she said. She worked on the buttons of his shirt.

"There's a thousand people outside."

She grinned. "I know. They're too loud to hear us." She reached inside his shirt to feel the warmth of his chest and went for another kiss. "Come on," she said. "You don't want to be the only one without any clothes on, do you?"

His fingers touched her, starting at the swell of her hips, slipping under the hem of her dress and around her bottom.

"Hey," he said. She laughed as his warm fingers touched bare skin.

"Surprise!"

He responded with a slight tent under his tuxedo pants. She knew she had him where she wanted him. Well, almost...

A sharp knock on the door froze them in place.

"Triana?"

Her mother!

Omar broke away faster than she had seen him move before. She beat him to the closet door and ushered him inside. Taking a deep breath, she paused before opening the dressing room door. She only let her mother see her face. She didn't want her to see the red flush of excitement on her neck.

"I'm changing," Triana announced.

"Hurry. We have reservations."

"I might be a while."

"How long does it take to change clothes? You got another party in there or something?"

"I'm...*decompressing.*"

"Don't keep your father waiting. Hurry up."

144 | BRIAN DRAKE

Her mother turned and walked into the backstage crowd. Triana let out a sigh and shut the door. She didn't let Omar out of the closet. Because Mom was right. If she kept her father waiting, he'd go from happy to total nuclear meltdown and what a way to ruin the night. She stripped off the dress, unzipped a gym bag, and took out appropriate undergarments. No surprises for anybody tonight after all. Her after party outfit hung on a wall hook, a simple blouse and slacks combo, decent heels, and a big jacket.

After dressing, she finally opened the closet.

Omar stood still. He looked nervous.

"Sorry, baby, next time."

"What do I do? We can't both leave the same dressing room."

Getting inside with all the confusion might have gone unnoticed. But she knew he was right. They had to space out the departure.

"Wait ten minutes."

Omar let out an exasperated sigh. Judging from the tent at his crotch, he'd need to wait longer than ten minutes. He found a chair in front of the makeup table. He ignored his reflection in the mirror.

"Good job tonight, honey," she said. She bent down to kiss his cheek.

"You, too."

"See you." Triana, her dressed folded into the gym bag, left him behind and hurried to catch up with her family.

Poor Omar. All revved up and nowhere to stick it.

She'd make it up to him next time.

They saw each other often. There was no secret to their relationship. But she kept a secret from him. He didn't know her father was a cartel boss. She'd managed to hide the fact from everybody she knew, and the deception wasn't always easy. The hardest part was coming up with an excuse for why she didn't introduce him to her family. *Gee, hon, my Dad is a narco who may get shot or arrested at any moment. Do you want to be there when it happens?*

She'd seen it too many times growing up. Other friends' fathers hadn't had the luck her father had. In the best case, only the police showed up in the middle of the night. In the worst cases, assassins kicked down the door. Sometimes, neither the law or competing narcos pulled the trigger. Sometimes, vigilantes did the job. The specter of *Los Pepes* still hovered over every cartel. The vigilantes who targeted Pablo Escobar set their sights on others. Randomly. One never knew if they hid within the shadows...

Deep down Triana knew her father was smarter than the not-so-lucky. The cops and competing narcos wouldn't have it easy when they targeted Antonio Panadero.

But she also feared backlash against *her* should anybody find out who her Daddy was.

It was one thing to love the man. Another thing entirely to expect regular people to accept her as one of them. Now that she had to leave the youth orchestra, it was more important than ever her secret remained safe.

She found her parents and Uncle Sal waiting on the steps outside. She took a few extra moments to hug a couple of stray orchestra mates and say good-bye. She promised to catch up with them at the after-party once she finished dinner. Her family wanted to celebrate with her, too.

Her father and Uncle Sal held the back door open for her. Her mother was already inside the black limousine with the tinted windows. She knew people were watching. She hoped they didn't make assumptions because of the limo. She wanted them to think her family had rented it for the night. She didn't want them to know it was her father's personal armored chariot.

"Very good, my darling," her father said, as she leaned into the doorway and joined her mother inside. Her father entered next. Then Uncle Sal.

"Yes," Uncle Sal said. He beamed at her. "Very good indeed. You were the best on stage."

She blushed and looked away. She didn't know how to respond.

30

THE NIGHTMARES KEPT RAVEN AWAKE.

He slept in one-to-two-hour bursts, snapping awake when the crackles of gunfire and the crash of explosions mingled with visions of his team's faces. He saw them all as the rockets tore their bodies apart. As he remained powerless to stop the massacre. Each time he awoke, he lay gasping for a few minutes, then waited for sleep to return. It usually did. For another hour or two.

They wouldn't leave him alone until he settled accounts. Avenged them. Then he could rest. Then the team—Ellison, Starkey, Pope, Chen, and Marshall—would join the ghosts of battles past. Where they'd have plenty of company. One big group to keep pushing him along the path of war without end. He'd been powerless when they died; he wasn't powerless now.

He groggily showered and dressed and went down for breakfast. Two cups of hearty black tea did little to revive him. But the pancake and egg breakfast helped a little. He bought a big Monster energy drink in the lobby gift shop to further take off the edge. He chugged half of it in the elevator ride back to his room. By the time he locked his door, it was almost gone. He felt a little more awake, but not much. And he'd pay for the drink with the jitters later.

Raven sat down and called Oscar Morey. Oscar didn't know about the results in Colombia. Raven had to tell him. He also had to stress he didn't blame Oscar for missing Kendrick Ward's link to bad actors like Panadero.

"Sam!" Oscar said as he picked up. "I've been wondering what happened."

"It went bad, Oscar," Raven began. He gave his friend a detailed account.

"Oh my God," Oscar said. "How did I miss—"

"The Ward stuff was DEA-specific. You couldn't have found it. I'm not blaming you. He fooled us both."

"Do you keep thinking about how you could have kept them alive?"

"If I don't, the nightmares do it for me."

"I get it. And I wish I had an answer for you. What are your plans?"

"I'm going to destroy this conspiracy."

"The DEA isn't going to like you."

"Hell with them. If they'd been nicer, especially what's-her-face, I might have cooperated in good faith."

"How can I help?" Oscar asked.

"I asked Clark for a rundown of the players, but I'd like to see if you can find anything he didn't. Especially on Yasmin Sevilla. I want to know where she is right now."

"I can answer the last question first. Hang on a minute."

Raven listened while Oscar worked a computer keyboard in the background. Did the old man ever leave his office? He seemed to be there every time Raven phoned. Not a bad thing, but he hoped his friend saw the sun now and then.

Oscar returned to the line. "Yasmina is fighting for control and rallying her father's people to her side. High casualties on all sides. There are four or five factions trying to take over. As for her location, she's at her home in Colombia."

"Send me the location."

"Sure. But, Sam—"

"Yes. I'm doing exactly what you're thinking."

"And when she finds out you killed her father?"

"I'll explain it to her."

Oscar laughed. "Right. Cartel leaders are reasonable people. She'll understand."

"She'll understand somebody else is the one who made it happen."

"She'll kill you anyway. Semantics doesn't matter to these people. And why the hell am I telling you what you already know?"

"I can't do it alone, Oscar. And I'm not calling in anybody else this time."

"You're nuts. You're nuts enough to pull it off, too."

"Send me her location, please," Raven said. "We'll see what happens."

"Anything else?"

"I'm in DC. I need travel documents in a name not my own. I know a few people here who can provide, but the DEA can find them if they look in my CIA file. Who do you know who is off the radar and can get what I need?"

"You paying cash?"

"I'm paying cash," Raven confirmed.

"I'll send you a name. Don't go saying it out loud."

"One and done. I don't expect to use this fellow again."

"It's a she. And she is an artist. She'll do whatever you need and take the best passport picture you've ever had."

"I'll be sure to update my real one with the new picture. Thanks, Oscar."

"Sam, I'm sorry as hell."

"I told you it's not your fault. I'll be in touch."

"All right," Oscar said. Raven ended the call.

He sat on the bed with the phone in his hand and stared at the carpet. He wondered why Oscar had asked about sleeping. He wondered what kept his friend up at night. He didn't like how Oscar hinted he'd have to live with the nightmares.

He had enough to live with already.

OSCAR SENT the name of his document fixer. Raven hit the street after 6 p.m., heading for Independence Avenue again. Oscar had also arranged the appointment and provided a pass code for Raven to use. He hadn't expected the cloak-and-dagger approach. What amused him more was Oscar's delight in telling him the code. It was as if he'd never had a chance to use something similar himself.

He was on his way to meet a tall redhead named Abby Alesis. Oscar provided no details about her. He only said she could get Raven the fake passport and travel documents he needed to get back into Colombia. And Raven hadn't asked. He didn't care. Only the mission mattered now. He needed to silence the nightmares.

What he did care about was arriving at Abby's nightclub without bringing the DEA with him.

He walked along Independence. He moved at a quick pace among the other pedestrians, people out for the evening. They were going to various restaurants along the road. Traffic was thick, too. Raven had his eyes on a cab, eventually. He needed to get the DEA team in sight first, then shake them via a "getaway car" and leave them standing still.

A quick glance back showed Black Jacket hustling to keep up Skull Cap wasn't in sight. They weren't trying to hide. It didn't hurt to let your subject know he was being followed; sometimes, there was no way to prevent discovery. But it made Raven's attempt at a dodge easier. *They should have changed the crew,* he thought. Had they done so, Raven would have to identify the new team before shaking them. This way, he knew who to look for. *Personnel shortages strike again.* Violence against them was still a no-no. Raven had no beef with the DEA. He put the surveillance squarely on Chandler. Patel went along because he was a follower. He hadn't impressed Raven during their short conversation. Except when he told Chandler to pipe down and informed Raven about the accountant.

He ducked down an alley and ran to the other side. Then he crossed the street ahead against traffic, stopped by a red light, and found another alley. He didn't run to the other side, but instead watched. He let the shadows cover him and tolerated the smell. A full Dumpster behind him stank; the effects of trash from the restaurant behind the wall. He saw no sign of Black Jacket or Skull Cap. Had he shaken them?

Raven went down to the other end and turned right. He wanted to talk a little more before grabbing a cab. He found a café with an outdoor sitting area. He stopped for a cup of tea and watched the street. He sat with his back to the front window. By the time he finished the tea, he knew he was clear. He paid, left the café, and hailed a cab. Hopping in the back, he gave the driver the address provided by Oscar and sat back and tried to relax. But he remained on edge. There was no relaxing right now. He was tense from lack of sleep, tense from the pressure of the mission. A private vendetta. *Soon. Very soon. Hang in there a little longer.*

A little longer.

He'd return to the battle zone and get even.

31

THE SKINNY CAB DRIVER LET HIM OUT HALF A BLOCK AWAY from the nightclub. Raven paid cash and hit the sidewalk again. He breezed through the crowd on the sidewalk. The other people were too wrapped up in their own lives, their own conversations, to notice him. He wished them well.

Abby Alesis owned "Abby's," and what Oscar had described as a "nightclub" was actually a quiet dinner venue. Brightly lighted, everybody dressed formally. Raven was actually *under* dressed in his jeans and light jacket. The greeter didn't tell him to leave. She was a stocky blonde in dark clothes, asked if he wanted a seat at the bar. He said no. He told her he was there to see Abby and had told to say it was raining in Glasgow. The greeter smiled, suggested he take a seat in the bar after all, and wait for somebody to get him. It wouldn't be Abby, she said, but one of her assistants. Raven made his way to the bar. The lights were lower. Patrons filled every stool at the bar. The assortment of leather chairs was almost full, too, but he found one along a mirrored wall. A passing waitress informed him she'd be with him in a moment. She carried a tray full of drinks to another table. Raven consulted the cocktail menu and wondered if he had enough time to order a gin-and-tonic. He decided the hell with it and did so when the waitress returned. She delivered two minutes later. The bartender went heavy on the gin, and Raven enjoyed the glow as he drank half down. It was only then that a man in a suit approached. The man told him Ms. Alesis had sent him, and asked Raven to follow. "Bring your drink," the man said.

Raven found Abby seated behind her desk in the back office. She told the escort to leave and the man in the suit shut the door on his way out. Abby Alesis smiled as Raven stood waiting in front of her cluttered desk. He swallowed more of his drink.

The office was small, her desk full of stacks of paperwork. Paintings hung on the walls, nice landscapes and portraits. Raven didn't recognize any of the work, but the artist knew how to paint a realistic picture. The paintings could have passed for photographs.

"Oscar tells me you need a passport and visa for Colombia," she said.

She dressed strikingly well in a form-fitting dress, low cut, thin straps over her shoulders. Freckles spotted her pale chest and crawled down her cleavage. She was pale all over, actually. The shock of long red hair highlighted her white skin.

"Correct," Raven said.

"I'm not cheap."

"You do the work yourself?"

"Yes. I'm a failed artist." She gestured at the walls. "Nobody wanted my paintings, but *everybody* wants my passports."

"These paintings are very good."

"Flattery won't get you any discounts."

"I'm serious."

154 | BRIAN DRAKE

"Sure," she said. She tapped a red fingernail on the arm of his chair.

Raven got back to business. "How much, and how long will it take?"

"Five grand for the passport and visa. And I'll be nice and give you the friends and family discount anyway, so no haggling. As for how long, I'll need a week. The visa paperwork takes the longest. I have a connection at the embassy who gets me the blanks. It may be forged, but they can't say you invented the thing using computer paper."

"Fine," Raven said. He was in no mood to haggle anyway. A week was too long, but there were other things to do while he waited.

He wanted to save Kendrick Ward for last. Taking him out first would only spook Antonio Panadero and make him run. Raven needed him to think he was still free and clear. He wanted Ward to feel a similar sense of security.

"Half in advance," the woman said.

"You think I'm carrying five grand on me?"

"Tomorrow, noon."

"Meet you here?"

"I'll meet you. Don't worry, Oscar told me where to find you."

"Did he also tell you I have friends tagging along?"

Abby Alesis frowned. "Feds?"

"DEA. I'm not on their Christmas card list."

"What do you suggest?"

"Show up like you own the place, and come up to my room."

"Okay."

"The money isn't at the hotel, either," Raven said. "Don't think you can send your buddy to find it while I'm sleeping."

"Who do you take me for?"

"One of Oscar's friends."

She tipped her head back and let out a hearty laugh.

"You know Oscar well," she said. "I'm not offended. I'll be at your room noon tomorrow. You'll be on your way to Colombia before you know it."

"Good. Thank you, Abby."

"What do I call you?"

"Raven. See you tomorrow."

He set the unfinished gin-and-tonic on the edge of her desk and found his way out. At five grand for the package, she could afford to cover his drink.

He sat in the back of another cab on his way to the hotel. The passing scenery held minor interest. There was nothing else to do but stare out the window and think.

Oscar had a point about dealing with Sevilla's daughter, Yasmina. She'd not hesitate to punch his ticket if she knew he led the murder squad. It was best to avoid her unless he created an approach that didn't include telling her of his involvement. Turn her into a proxy fighter on his behalf. She'd be motivated enough.

When he entered the hotel lobby, he spotted Black Jacket seated off to the side. He glared at Raven. Raven smiled and waved. *Not my fault you can't hang...*

He wondered where Black Jacket's friend, Skull Cap, was hiding. He was probably outside in a car.

Raven shut the door to his hotel room. He thought about calling room service for dinner, then decided no. He wanted to go to bed. If he had longer to sleep, even off and on, it might help the next day.

32

KENDRICK WARD SAT IN FRONT OF THE COMPUTER SCREEN ON his desktop. He'd locked the door to his home office and asked his wife not to disturb him. But what condition he'd be in when he finally exited the den remained to a mystery. Nobody came out of a chat with Panadero without appearing as if they'd been through the wringer.

Antonio Panadero's face filled the computer screen. They were in the middle of the Zoom call. Ward didn't like what the cartel boss had to say in response to his opener. *Should have kept my mouth shut.*

Ward was still nervous about Sam Raven showing up. And said so.

"I have had enough of your so-called concern," Panadero said. His voice rose, peaking through the computer speakers. "You're behaving like a child, and if I were there, I'd beat sense into you. Fox will stay with you until further notice. Yes? Is this satisfactory? Will you shut the fuck up now?"

Ward knew it wasn't a question.

Panadero wanted a full-time observer in the Ward home. Fox wouldn't be there to guard, but spy. Ward gave the big boss the perfect excuse. He'd have had to find one had Ward said nothing about Raven. *Great. Nice job, turkey.* Ward's gut told him he was right; he also knew there was no way to refuse.

"Good idea," he said. He took a breath to suppress his true reaction. "Yes, Fox will be fine."

"Then we have finished the subject of Sam Raven," Panadero stated. "The man is *dead*, Ken. D-E-A-D. You're behaving as if he were the boogeyman. You make me wonder if I made the right choice in selecting you as my representative."

"No need for doubts, Tony," Ward said. "I'm fine. But I'd much prefer we had a body to know for sure."

"Not having a body doesn't mean your enemy is still alive. There have been plenty of examples of the opposite. Now, we have other matters to discuss. More *important* matters. Where are you with our first contact meeting?"

Ward cleared his throat and shifted in his big chair. This was where he'd show Panadero his true value once again. The big boss would leave the call with no doubts about Ward's abilities. He'd bring the required connections together. He was a master at getting opposite sides to the negotiating table. His victory at home would expand Panadero's reach and his fortune.

"I have an appointment with the Ludavico Syndicate in New York City. I'll be seeing the old man's kid—who will soon take over, by the way. The father is going to step down and retire to Florida. This may be a one-and-done, Tony. They're already seeing a shortage and it's causing problems on the street. Sevilla's people aren't bringing product into the US any longer."

Panadero laughed. "Too busy killing themselves over a worthless empire."

"Ludavico controls distribution up and down the East

Coast," Ward said, "except for one area. He may be willing to move on the territory he doesn't control should our volume be high enough. I have my presentation prepared. Would you like to see it?"

"No. Let me know when Fox arrives. I will direct him to be at your house by this evening."

Panadero vanished from the screen. Ward turned off the computer and sat heavily in his seat. He had not wanted Fox assigned to the house. He'd now have to explain the matter to his wife, and he'd already spun a tale about the five other men roaming the grounds. Now he had to spin another. After a few minutes' thought, he came up with a story she'd go for.

His wife, Maddie, wasn't the most involved person since their daughter died. She preferred others do her thinking for her. She focused on distractions like gardening and her assorted hobbies. She'd raised her kids; what more did the world want from her? And what more was she required to give? Ward could use her attitude to his advantage. In this case.

Maddie hadn't always been "checked out" on the rest of the world. They all went through a chance when Francie died. Her loss affected them in various ways, none taking it the same way. Maddie pulled back from life; Ward dove into work. He couldn't say what his other kids did.

The two children still alive were out of the house. His daughter Phoebe, the youngest, had recently started college. Ward didn't approve of her taste in men. She kept bringing home free-boating losers. He wanted her with somebody more straight-and-narrow. Somebody with a future. Somebody like him, with a head for business.

His son, Josh, was an engineering major. Due to graduate in six months. Several prestigious firms were already courting him. He was proud of the boy.

And there was Francine, for whom he no longer had to worry. She was where they'd left her in the cemetery after the drug overdose ended her life.

He hadn't wanted to stir up memories of Francine. He wanted to forget the horrible night when the hospital called. But he'd also known telling her story to Raven would be the way into Raven's head. There'd be no way for the man to refuse the mission when he learned how Ward's past mirrored his own. It was what had kept him aboard when whoever it was on the mercenary team made him ask about Zac Fox.

Ugh, what to do? he wondered. He didn't dislike Fox. The man was handy to have around, when he was around; Ward also liked it when he went his own way. But now he'd be a full-time guest. He'd want a room to himself. The other three guards shared the detached mother-in-law suite in the back of the house. Fox would want to be in the main house in case anything happened. He'd be at the front line of defense. Ward laughed without humor. Was the house he'd worked so hard for now a military camp? What had he done?

He left his desk and opened the door to go find his wife.

As he headed for the staircase, he remembered the days when he hadn't been a stooge to the local mafia. Or a cartel boss twenty-five hundred miles away. The descent into personal corruption happened gradually. His business, early on, required a favor or two from the local gangsters. They, in turn, asked for favors of their own. One thing led to another. Like many other situations in life, one never noticed the changes taking place until it was too late to turn around. Ward knew it was far too late to tell anybody no. They had their hooks in him and no mistake. What he had now was the illusion of his own sovereignty. He was wealthy, but at a cost. And since Francie died, the money wasn't worth anything to him. He wanted his daughter back, his family intact. He wanted to die an old man with three kids and a wife at his bedside. He didn't want to look at the empty place-setting on the table during Thanksgiving and Christmas. He didn't want the reminder of how he'd failed to protect her when she needed him most.

He found Maddie out back, in the garden, on her knees tending to her rose bushes. He stood on the patio and watched. He didn't want to disturb her. But Fox was on his way. He couldn't avoid the conversation.

He crossed the grass and called her name.

33

CLARK WILSON WAS HAVING A QUIET DAY WHEN THE telephone on his desk rang. He noted it was an outside line, but didn't recognize the number. He closed the file on his lap and picked up.

"Yes?"

"Wilson? Hollie Chandler, DEA."

Wilson frowned. The DEA and Special Activities often coordinated anti-drug efforts. But only a few specific people had his telephone number. As a rank-and-file agent, Hollie Chandler wasn't one of them. And the DEA woman sounded mad.

"You're not supposed to have this number, Ms. Chandler."

"*Mrs.*," she snapped. "And never mind how I got it. You and I need to talk about your friend."

"Excuse me?"

"Sam Raven. He's going back on his word and I want to know what he's doing."

"I have no idea what you're talking about, Mrs. Chandler."

"You're a liar. We have people watching him in DC. They saw *you* go to his hotel. He's since evaded them twice. Tell me what he's doing. Better yet, remind him he promised to *back off*. Or there will be consequences."

"I have no idea what you're talking about, Mrs. Chandler. Nor should you be talking to me like this. If you have a problem, go through the usual channels to sort it out."

"Tell him to stop."

"I have no idea what you're talking about," Wilson said for the third time. And the final time. "Good-bye."

Wilson hung up.

Dammit, Raven. He shook his head. He'd have to get in touch with his pal. In the meantime, he had a report to finish reading. Raven could take care of himself in the meantime. He tried to resume reading, but couldn't focus. He needed fresh air. He left his desk to take a break.

IN HER OFFICE IN BOGOTA, Hollie Chandler slammed down the telephone in disgust.

"No luck?" Bradley Patel said from the other side of the room. He sat behind his desk same as she did, but his face wasn't beet red.

"He better tell Raven or I'm finding a way to let Sevilla's daughter know he's the man she wants."

"You wouldn't."

"I absolutely would. I'm not going to let him ruin everything we've worked for."

"Hollie."

"*What?*"

"You need to go home."

"What kind of shit is that, Brad?"

"Your husband called again last night, didn't he?"

"None of your *business*, Brad. Stay out of my private life."

"You're blaming Raven for something you yourself are

going to do if you aren't careful. You'll ruin everything by making poor decisions. I can only cover you so much."

"I'll tell you what I told my husband. We're so close to winning, I only need a little more time. He acts like he can't take care of our children by himself."

Patel shook his head. "No, he wants you there because you're a *team*, Hollie. You can't expect him to handle your son alone."

"He doesn't need me."

"Your *son* does."

"Stop it," she said. "I want our people in Bogota alerted to Raven. He might come back here and start shit. They are to intercept him or *shoot him* if he won't cooperate." Hollie rose from her desk and grabbed a few files, which she stuffed into a briefcase. She shut the lid and snatched her purse from a drawer. "I'll see you tomorrow."

"Go home, Hollie," Patel said. But he was talking to her back. She was already through the office doorway.

He sighed. She'd given an order, and he had to follow instructions. All he needed to do was write a simple email memo, so he set his current work aside and typed the memo. He sent it out to the field personnel and included relevant details about Raven and a file photo. He didn't need her yelling and screaming any more than she had already. He didn't understand why she wasn't going home. Colombia wasn't so important to require the kind of sacrifice she was making. If she insisted on staying, she'd have to deal with the inevitable damage sure to result.

Best not to dwell on it, he decided. She told him it was none of his business. Fine. He returned to his work.

ANTONIO PANADERO STOOD on the upper balcony of his home. He faced the back side and stared at the tennis court and neighboring swimming pool. Both were immaculate, as he demanded. But he'd used neither in so long he couldn't remember the last time. A game of tennis with Sal would be a good antidote to the stress of the current operation. Yes, Sevilla was gone, a major obstacle removed. But there were other problems, and future problems to anticipate and solve. There were also any number of problems sure to arise they had no way to see coming. Such was the nature of life.

As if sensing his thoughts, Sal Costa stepped up beside him. "Thinking of our last game?"

"How long ago was it?"

"About three months, I think."

"Who won? You or me?" Panadero said.

"Your daughter won. She played both of us."

Panadero laughed. "Sure. I let her win."

"Not even you would let her win, Tony."

"Let's pretend. It hurt the ego more than I'd like to admit."

"We aren't busy now. Shall we play?"

"You'd win. My head is elsewhere."

"What's the problem?" Costa said.

Panadero explained the call with Ward. He talked about Ward's worry over Raven and sending Zac Fox to the business man's house.

"I was going to find a way to send Fox anyway," Panadero said. "I want eyes and ears there for when Ward begins his meetings. His worry gave me all the excuse I needed."

"So what's the problem?"

"I think I'm worried about Raven, too." Panadero turned to Costa. "What do you say? More troopers here? Just in case?"

"More troops and a lock down. Nobody in or out for at least two days. If Ward is taking meetings, we're a short time away from fulfilling our goals. And reaching our goals will bring trouble from other quarters. From Yasmina Sevilla, perhaps."

"And we'll have a whole other fight on our hands."

"There will be resistance from her, for sure. Once she gets organized."

"We should have killed her, too."

"Still can."

Panadero shook his head. "Let me think it over. She may be useful to us as-is, for now."

"And *how*, exactly?"

"She's fighting for control of her father's organization. Those who want it for themselves are fighting her instead of us. For now, the situation favors us. When it is strategically sensible to remove Yasmina Sevilla from the land of the living, we will do so. I do not sense now is the time."

"Fair enough," said Costa. "Where should I call our extra support troops from?"

Panadero looked off in the distance, thinking over his answer. He didn't want to pull from sensitive areas like the farms because of their vulnerability. Any decrease in security might tempt bandits who wanted to steal his crops.

He could pull from processing plants, though. Those weren't as "soft" as farms. He told Costa his decision, and Costa nodded.

"We'll make it happen. I'll direct them to be here by late this afternoon."

"And the lock down idea is good, too," Panadero said. "I don't want anybody leaving for seventy-two hours. We'll reevaluate then."

Costa nodded again. "Anything else?"

Panadero smiled. "Maybe next week, I'll take you up on that tennis game."

Costa grinned. "I look forward to it."

Costa departed. Panadero welcomed the solitude once again. He stared at the mountains in the distance, the big green giants he'd known since childhood. Everything around those mountains changed; they did not. They paid little attention to life around them, because it was all temporary. Panadero knew he was a speck of dust in comparison, but for as long as possible, he wanted to be as big as they were. With the East Coast drug connection secured, he surely would be. Then the mountains wouldn't look so big anymore.

34

WORD OF THE RESTRICTIONS SPREAD FAST. One member of the household had no intention of obeying her father's order.

Triana's bedroom was on the third floor of the mansion. The wrap-around walkway on the rest of the floor did not extend to her bedroom. She wished he had a doorway to walk out and enjoy the view, but had to settle for a window instead. According to her mother, Papa didn't want his men wandering past her door on their rounds. He was afraid they'd try and sneak a peek at her, especially when she hit the teenage years. She thought it was silly. Her father's troops knew her well and treated her with respect. The guard leader, Mateo, always made sure the boss's daughter had the protection she needed. But maybe her father knew something she didn't. It was one of those things she didn't want to ask about because her father would get mad and blow his top.

He was going to get mad and explode anyway when he found out she was gone.

She had a date with Omar in the city.

She'd asked her mother, why the lock down? When the extra troops arrived at four in the afternoon, they both shared looks of concern. The armed men arrived in two trucks, and Mateo assigned them to march around the perimeter. Her father only said he was "taking precautions", but didn't elaborate. Were they in danger? She thought back to the deadly lullaby of *Los Pepes* when her father spoke of "precautions." This wasn't the first time.

She'd be taking a risk leaving the house, then, but she had to make it up to Omar. She owed him from the night of the concert.

Triana picked out the right outfit. They were going to have a quiet dinner and go dancing. She stood in front of the mirror trying to decide between a red dress or a black one. Both were similar spaghetti-strap affairs with low cuts and skirts "just long enough". She'd need stockings for sure. If she went with black, she could hit the red lipstick hard and make the outfit pop. She chose the red dress. She wanted to stand out and have all eyes on her. Her lipstick choice was an easy one, too. She'd go with a light peach color. It wouldn't clash, wouldn't be obvious; the shade would blend in and be... *mysterious*. She laughed as she tossed the red on her bed and hung the black dress in the closet.

A shower, makeup, she stepped into the dress...and pulled on a long coat. It wasn't a heavy coat, but long enough to cover what she wore beneath. She checked her watch. Almost six p.m. Time to go. She had to sneak out, and felt giddy with anticipation.

Her mother and father and Uncle Sal were in the dining room; most of the house was quiet. She moved casually through the lower floor to a connecting walkway. The enclosed hall led to the detached garage. She kept her car there, a sensible Jeep with the roof attached. She didn't bother turning on the lights as she fished the key fob from her small purse. The low lights in the garage let her see where she was going. She traveled past her father's collection of obnoxious sports cars without a glance. Her Jeep sat at the end of the row.

"Miss?"

She stopped, startled by the voice. She looked around, checking shadows for the man the voice belonged to. The guard, cradling his weapon, stepped out from between the second row of cars across from her.

"Where are you going, miss?" the man said. The low light cast a shadow over his face. She couldn't identify him and didn't recognize his voice.

"Out for a bit. My father knows."

"Your father said nobody leaves for two days."

"It's okay." She started forward again.

"Miss."

"I told you, my father *knows*, okay? Go away." Her heels tapped as she walked faster.

The guard said nothing more and she hurried to the Jeep, and climbed behind the wheel. She hit the garage door opener fastened to the visor above. The engine fired at the first twist of the key and she exited, hitting the button again to close the door behind her.

Her headlamps shined bright, carving out a path ahead. The paved lane to the main gate wasn't straight. She had to follow the curve and keep her speed down. She didn't see any guards assembling behind her, but knew, by now, the man in the garage had sounded the alarm.

Another remote on the visor opened the main gate. She had to stop while it swung open. And it swung so s-l-o-w-l-y she wanted to scream. Before it was all the way open, she twisted the wheel, rumbled through the gap, and onto the mountain road. A left turn, and a step on the gas. The Jeep picked up speed. She was on her way and leaving the mansion behind. She'd deal with her father later. He might yell and scream but he'd never lay a hand on her.

PANADERO ROSE from the dining table and regarded the trooper coldly. He pressed his lips together in a tight line, his face twisted in anger.

"She did *what?*"

The guard stuttered. "Took her Jeep and drove off. I couldn't stop her."

"Couldn't? You didn't try."

Beside the guard stood the chief of security, Mateo Ferreira. He towered over the guard and was big and bulky with a broad chest, thick arms and legs, and thick black hair.

Panadero approached the guard and punched him in the gut. Marina yelped; the guard doubled over and fell on the floor.

To Mateo, Panadero snapped, "She'll go to her boyfriend's place. Bring her back. Drag her back by her hair if you must. Do *not* fail."

Mateo nodded, and stepped over the fallen guard as he departed. The man on the floor tried to suck in a breath but only made choking sounds.

Panadero reached down, grabbed the man, and hauled him to his feet. The guard tried to stand but still had to bend over. He held onto his belly.

"You fail me again, and you'll beg me to punch you. But instead, I'll hang you by your *balls*. Understand?"

The guard nodded. He kept sucking breath in short gasps.

"What kind of man are you to let a little girl get the better of you?"

The guard gasped. His face was red.

"Get out of my sight."

The guard clutched his weapon close and hurried away.

Panadero cleared his throat, resumed his seat at the table, and started eating again. He ignored the glare of his wife. And the look of shock from Salvador Costa.

35

Triana drove to Omar's apartment. He shared the space with three other roommates. Like all young men on their own, they barely kept the place clean. There were always odds and ends scattered about. She was afraid to use the bathroom when she visited for a length of time. It was often filthy. Luckily, Omar learned quick. He made sure the bathroom was spotless before she showed up.

Tonight was one of those nights. He must have cleaned thoroughly. As she stepped through the doorway, she smelled the lingering bleach. She planned to come back with him after dinner, but wasn't going to stay all night.

He gave her a kiss and they hugged. With his roommates nearby, they weren't going to do more. Omar had dressed up, too. His black suit fit him well; his black shoes reflected a high polish.

"You ready?" he asked.

"I'm starving." Triana wanted to tell him how she almost didn't make it off her father's property; she held back. She had to behave as if her family was normal.

They departed in Omar's car. He drove an old Honda

with worn out seats. The passenger seat had a tear in it, but not much foam had leaked out yet.

Omar took her to Andrés Carne de Res, a favorite restaurant of theirs. Omar had taken her there on their first date, and they went back often.

Thick bars blocked off the outdoor seating area. The thick beams were wrapped barber-pole style with yellow tape. A short line of diners waited to get inside—the ones who hadn't called ahead to reserve seating. Omar told the doorman they had reservations, and they walked under the arched neon sight. The sign burned bright with a low hum.

The hostess led them through the crowded and noisy dining room. Servers carrying trays navigated the narrow walking space with ease. There were two seating options. Near the bar sat wooden tables with wood-topped stools on metal legs. More comfortable seating included booths on the other wall. Up two flights of stairs was the second floor, and more seating. The hostess led them up the two flights of stairs to the upper dining room and sat them in a booth.

Both floors of the restaurant were heavily decorated on the walls and ceiling. To the cynic, the place resembled a junk yard. The most eclectic (i.e.: tacky) collection of junk hung from the ceiling; no space spared. Identifying individual pieces was a great way to spend time waiting for food. And on a date where there wasn't much talking at first, pointing out this piece of that piece filled the awkward gaps.

The hostess provided menus, told them their server would be with them soon, and departed. They opened the menus.

"What are we sharing tonight?" Omar said.

Andrés Carne de Res offered big portions of grilled meats and traditional Colombian dishes. Ordering individually was a one-way ticket to a full take-away container for the next day. Sharing plates saved money. Omar wasn't rich, and

Triana had to hide how much money she had access to as well.

"Did you read the reviews of the concert?" he asked.

"No."

"Four and five stars all around," he said with a grin. "They didn't mention you and me, but they liked the show. It's the best notice we've ever gotten."

She said, "Maybe I'm wrong."

"About what?"

"Our composition needing work."

"It's fine."

"I guess."

"I was thinking," he said, "we should make a recording. Take it around and see if we can get a record deal."

"Really?"

"Can you imagine the two of us on a world tour?"

She looked for something to fiddle with. The forks and knives were wrapped in a white napkin. She scanned the menu instead, but didn't register what the words said.

"Are you okay?" he asked.

"It's too much to think about," she said. She put down the menu. "Having to leave the orchestra is like graduating from high school. I don't know what to do next."

"We have an opportunity," he said. "There's no reason not to take advantage."

"Do you think we can?"

He leaned closed. "I *know* we can."

"I don't know."

"What else are you going to do? Get a job? Go to university?"

"I was thinking of applying to Pontificia."

Pontificia Universidad Javeriana was the go-to university for performing arts.

"But why?" he said. "What do you have to learn?"

"There's *always* something more to learn," she said. "We don't know everything, Omar."

"I want to get out of Bogota and make money," he said.

"What if we both attended?" she said.

Omar sat back. He didn't reply. She tried to smile.

Their waitress arrived. They ordered drinks but wanted more time to consult the menu.

"What do you want to eat?" he said.

"Can we talk more about this later?"

"If we keep putting things off till later, life will make our choices for us. We have to be pro-active. This isn't something to wait for."

Deep down she knew he was right. But stepping out on her own...it was scary. She led a sheltered life. She'd never had to work for anything on her own. Her father provided for every need. Would he support her trying to make a career as a musician?

Would it be harder to keep her secret? Being in the public eye meant exposure. Paparazzi. The press. Scrutiny. They'd want to know where she came from. They'd want to know about her family. She might hide for four years at a university, but the threat would always linger.

But Omar wanted an answer. She had to tell him something. And soon.

OMAR GRINNED as he shut the door to his bedroom. Triana had a bigger smile on her face.

It was time to make up for the night of the concert...

They had each other half undressed when a big crash stopped them. Omar's roommates yelled in the other room; one of them was cut off mid-sentence by a punch. A loud smack of a fist against flesh.

"Oh, no," Triana said. She hurried to get back in her clothes.

"What's going on?"

A knock at the door.

"Wait!" Triana shouted.

"What's happening?"

"I can't—"

The doorknob rattled. A heavy shoulder slammed into the door, forcing it open. Part of the door jamb splintered as the big man stepped into the room. He reached for the light switch on the wall like he'd lived in the apartment all his life.

"Dammit, Mateo!" Triana shouted. She pulled up the last strap and started looking for her shoes. Her dress had some wrinkles now, but she didn't bother with them.

Omar, zipping his pants but leaving his shirt untucked, looked at the man in the doorway.

He was big and broad and looked bored. He spoke to Triana. "You have disappointed your father, Triana."

"Fuck you!" she shouted.

The big man cracked half a smile.

"What is this?" Omar said. "*Who* is this?"

"Do you know who her father is?" the big man said.

"We haven't met," Omar said.

The big man chuckled.

So Omar asked Triana.

"He's a *narco*, okay? This is Mateo, one of his goons." She pulled on her last shoe and grabbed her coat. "I guess we'll try again later."

"Triana—" Omar began.

Mateo Ferreria grabbed Triana's left arm. "Go now. Talk later."

She tried to pull away, but he held tight. "No more games, little girl."

"Kill yourself, Mateo. Even *Jesus* hates you."

She went with him. He didn't say another word. Omar watched them leave the apartment. One of his roommates stood dumbfounded, looking from Omar to the now-closed door. The other was on the floor groaning. Omar ran to him.

Triana's father was a *narco*?

He wasn't sure what to think as he looked at his fallen roommate's face, and the red welt growing there.

36

SALVADOR COSTA TAPPED ON THE DOOR OF PANADERO'S DEN. The guard beside the door didn't stop him; in fact, the guard moved out of Costa's way. Panadero yelled for Costa to enter. Costa did so, and shut the door with a hard push. He carried a tablet computer and wore a worried expression.

Panadero recognized Costa's distress right away.

"What's wrong, Sal?"

"The DEA's moving on your accountant."

Panadero half rose from behind his desk. Costa showed him the tablet. "These pictures just came through. Here are the two agents, Patel and Chandler, talking to him."

Panadero took hold of the tablet and began scrolling through the shots. The surveillance crew had snapped each shot at a different angle from across a street. The pictures showed a run-down motel and the accountant, Saúl Elvira, entering a room. Another shot showed the two DEA agents arriving and going into the same room. Later shots showed the agents departing, with the last showing Elvira's exit.

"I'd like to know what they talked about," Costa said.

"We know what they talked about," Panadero said. "How

to get access to my accounts, trace my money and freeze my finances. Cripple the organization. Then make their moves militarily." Panadero scrolled back to the beginning to flip through the pictures a second time. "They were smart to wait, but we were smarter, Sal. We never stopped watching."

"What do you want to do?"

Panadero handed back the tablet. "He didn't go with them. What does that suggest?"

"Preliminary conversation. He has things to think about. We can kill him now, if you want."

"Sit down, Sal."

Costa moved to the chair in front of Panadero's desk. The cartel boss closed his computer file and turned his chair to face Costa.

"Let's run down the options and possibilities," Panadero said. "One, we kill him now. What happens? Worse case?"

"Dead man's switch. On his death, information on your accounts will go to the DEA or military and they get what they want anyway."

"Two, we do nothing. What happens?"

"They bring him in, he hands over the data, and they require a court order to freeze the accounts."

"Which gives us—"

"Time to move the money, especially if they use one of our judges."

"They'll vet them first," Panadero said, "if they haven't already."

Costa laughed. "Needle in a hay stack."

"Or…"

Costa raised an eyebrow.

Panadero smiled. "We send a message. The kind of message they'll never forget."

"I don't know if I like this."

"Let them bring him in, then attack their headquarters. Kill them all."

"Tony—"

"You have to admit it will be *spectacular*."

"It's stupid. They'll only come after us harder once the smoke clears."

Panadero shrugged. "A lot can change while they recover. They won't come at us overnight."

"I don't think—"

"They want to hurt *me*, Sal. They want to hurt *all* of us. If we wipe them out, they may even think twice."

Costa shifted in his seat. Panadero's temper was getting the best of him. Again. As always.

"I can't recommend such action," Costa said. "Even by proxy."

"We're not hiring mercenaries this time," Panadero said. "No, I want them to hurt. I want them to *bleed*. Let's make them bleed, Sal."

Costa stared at his friend.

"Are you going to listen to me, or do I find somebody who will?"

Costa took a deep breath. "It will be done, Tony. Under protest."

"Protest all you want; you know I'm right."

"We'll see." Costa rose to leave. He headed for the door.

"I expect a battle plan by tonight," Panadero called out.

"You'll have it," Costa told him. He left the den and pulled the door shut. The guard outside raised an eyebrow. He'd heard everything. Costa shook his head. The guard said nothing. Costa went on his way. He had a map to consult, pictures of the DEA headquarters to study. He needed to draft a battle plan whether he liked it or not.

He didn't want to be on the receiving end of Tony's wrath if he didn't comply.

RAVEN HAD eyes on him as soon as he cleared customs.

The false documents provided by Oscar's fixer, the redheaded Abby Alesis, raised no alarms. He'd changed his hair color from dark to blonde, and added a mustache and glasses. It wasn't much of a disguise, but the look matched his new passport photo. He knew from experience he didn't need a drastic disguise to fool casual observers. But he knew the DEA was in the crowd as he waited for his luggage; he knew they were looking at him. There was too much he couldn't change. His height, for one. His build, for another. No matter what his face showed, he had the makeup of a man who knew how to take care of himself.

He collected his single suitcase; his carry-on rode over his right shoulder. As he headed for the exit, he saw them. Two men picking up his trail without a second thought. Outside, it was hot and busy. Cars like the sidewalk; people getting in and out of the vehicles. A jumble of voices and jet noises. Raven broke right for a line of curbside taxis. Two familiar faces emerged from a cluster of young travelers and stopped him in his tracks.

"Nice mustache, Mr. Raven," Hollie Chandler said. Bradley Patel stood behind her. Raven glanced over his shoulder. The other two men from inside stopped behind him.

"You going to come with us, or make trouble?" Hollie said.

Raven turned to her. "I'll take a ride with you, sure."

The DEA agents led him to a black Suburban. He stowed his bags in the back, and joined them inside. The SUV merged into traffic. At least it was quiet inside, and not a bumpy ride.

He watched as Bogota flashed by through the tinted

windows. It was another warm day, and the palm trees stretched to the sky. A few clouds today. White against rich blue. Raven wondered why some parts of the world had bluer sky than other parts. It was the same sky, right? But in some places he'd visited, the blue appeared washed out, lighter; not so in Colombia. He wished the tinted windows didn't dilute the color.

Hollie Chandler sat on his left; Patel on the right. The other two agents sat in the far back row.

"What are we going to do with you, Mr. Raven?" Hollie said. "You gave us your word."

"I know."

"Yet here you are."

"Yeah."

"What if I told you the accountant has agreed to work with us? It's true. We made the arrangements. He's coming in with all of the data we need. We will freeze Panadero out of his money and a make him a sitting duck for what's next."

"Prison isn't good enough, Mrs. Chandler."

"You want him at the end of your gun and all that."

"Even you should understand the need to settle a score."

"Oh, I get it," she said. "But we do it by the book. We don't go around *murdering* people."

"Even if they deserve it?"

"It's not up to us to decide," she said.

"Hence the problem with law enforcement, and why I'd never have made a good police officer."

"No, you wouldn't have," she said. "Police officers are taught discipline. You have none."

"We'll see," he said.

They continued the ride in silence.

TRIANA PANADERO FACED her mother across a small table. They were in the food court of the Multiplaza Bogota, a large shopping center. But they weren't alone. Her father's goon, Mateo Ferreria, sat at another table nearby. Her father refused to let them off the property without the escort. His stupid lockdown had come and gone with no rhyme or reason. The estate resembled an armed camp with all the troops. There was nowhere to talk privately, and Triana had a lot on her mind.

"Omar dumped me," she said. She started to sob. Grabbing a tissue from her purse, she dabbed her eyes.

Her mother, Marina, watched with sympathetic eyes. There wasn't much to say.

Triana continued. "He told me he can't be with somebody who has a criminal for a father." She sniffed. "And he did it over a text message. Can you believe that? Wouldn't answer my calls."

"I'm sorry, hon."

"He told me he loved me." Another sniffle. "If he really did, why is he breaking it off?"

Marina pressed her lips together.

"I guess lying didn't help," her daughter continued. "You think?" She forced a laugh. "Is this my fault?"

"What do you think?" Marina said.

"I don't lie as well as Dad, I guess. What do I do now?"

"Find a way to continue," her mother said. "It's what we do when life doesn't work out."

"I don't want things to not work out."

"We don't have a choice sometimes. You can't force people to do things. Despite what your father thinks."

Triana looked down at her coffee cup. The steaming liquid held no answers either.

"Nothing's stopping you from going to university now," Marina said. "Do you still want to go?"

"I don't know what I want."

"For now, do nothing. Rest and get over this. After a few weeks you'll have a clearer head."

"I don't want to end up a cartel wife," Triana said. "Is that all I have to look forward to?"

"You can have whatever life you make for yourself," Marina said.

"Really? With that *thug* over there watching us? You think Dad will ever let me go?"

"Your father likes to control things, yes. He likes to control the people in *his* life."

"Like you and Uncle Sal."

Her mother nodded.

"What do I do?" Triana asked again.

Her mother reached for one of her hands and took hold. The grasp felt good. There might not be any answers right now, but Triana knew they'd come.

37

KENDRICK WARD CHECKED HIS WATCH FOR THE UMPTEENTH time. Zac Fox, the bearded gangster go-between, noticed from up front.

"We're on time, Mr. Ward."

Ward tugged the cuff of his blazer over his Rolex.

"This traffic is awful," he said.

"It's typical. Don't worry. We'll be there. And if we're a few minutes late, what are they gonna do?"

"I don't want to be late. I don't care if they have nowhere else to go. There will find somebody to turn to for supply if we don't make this deal. And then it's my ass."

"You have a point," Fox said.

Ward wanted to curse the big man, but held his tongue. It wouldn't have solved anything. And he needed the big man on his side even though he'd rather not have him around at all.

Fox had settled into the guest room at the Ward house. The story Ward fed his wife took hold. She appreciated how Fox corralled the other guards and made sure they earned their keep. They patrolled, took care of their own cooking, and did their best to stay out of the way. They for sure kept clear of Mrs. Ward's rose garden.

Ward tapped a foot nervously and turned his attention to the street. It had taken them forty-five minutes to travel two blocks. The gridlock they sat in made it seem like it would be forty-five more before they reached the supper club. The Ludavico representatives were waiting. Ward hoped his prediction of a "one and done" meeting proved true. He didn't want to spend a lot of time taking meetings with gangsters trying to establish the new drug pipeline. The Ludavico's had worked with Sevilla. They had the infrastructure in place; anybody else was building from scratch. He'd find another client, if need be, but it would waste a lot of time and money. And keep him from his real work.

Of course, if things worked out, he'd soon not have to worry about his "real work" ever again.

"How far are we from the club?" Ward asked.

"You can almost see it from here. On the left, near the end of the block."

Ward tried to see what Fox pointed out, but a bus inched into his field of view.

The Raven problem worried him less and less every day. There'd been no sign of him coming back to life. Tony must have been correct. Raven may have survived the rocket attack, but he died elsewhere. He knew enough about Raven to realize he'd have come back with guns blazing had he the ability to do so.

Traffic moved forward. Ward began to relax. Almost there.

———

WARD AND FOX walked through the door of the Three Note Supper Club. A man named Eddie Ludavico, the brother of the man who ran the Ludavico syndicate, opened the club in the 1930s. He'd booked only the best jazz musicians from around the world, but they'd played to the white-only audience. Nowadays the club was open to anybody. The only catch was the cost. The club wasn't cheap. They served high-end food prepared by a Michelin Star chef.

The club only had room for fifty people. Paintings lined the walls, positioned under lit arches. The light brought out the colors of each piece, even under their glass protection. Ward recognized one or two famous paintings that he figured were reproductions. Under the paintings was a wall-length bench seat, wrapped in red leather. Table and chairs opposite. Open tables occupied the center of the room. The empty bandstand promised a good time on nights when performers played. The long bar housed more bottles, and the biggest mirror, Ward had ever seen.

"Welcome to my grandfather's club," said a young man who approached the pair. Ward smiled and stepped forward with his hand out. "I'm Ethan Ludavico," the young man continued. He wore a dark tight-fitting suit which showed off his trim physique. His lightly-stubbled jaw and dark eyes gave him a striking appearance.

"Kendrick Ward," the businessman said. They shook hands. "This is my associate, Zac Fox."

Ethan Ludavico shook hands with the bearded man. His face changed a little. He'd gone from superior to cautious. He knew Fox wasn't a man to cross. Which meant Ward had more power than the dude realized. Ward smiled at the thought. He wanted the young buck to think *exactly* that.

"And this is my associate, Gunner Osborne," Ludavico said. He introduced another young man who sized up Fox before Ward. He shook hands with both. He wasn't as big as Fox, but looked like he possessed the ability to handle himself in a fight. Ward didn't want to find out one way or another. He didn't want any trouble at all. He hoped the two made men had the same idea.

"Please, be my guests," Ethan Ludavico said. He gestured to a corner table along the wall. He and Osborne took the leather bench side while Ward and Fox took the chairs. The polished wood table between them had a lit candle in the center. A waiter came over with a tray of martinis. Ward accepted with gladness. A little lubricant wouldn't hurt at all. Fox took his glass and set it in front of him but didn't touch it a second time.

Ludavico opened.

"I hope you can solve our supply problem. Our people on the street are down to the last of their supplies. We need to get more product out and fast. What do you propose?"

Ward waited to reply. Ludavico asked no questions about Sevilla; he wasn't surprised. All he wanted was a steady supply of narcotics. He didn't care who sold him the drugs. One cartel was the same as another. They were all expendable, replaceable, non-entities in the grand scheme. The realization sent a chill up Ward's neck.

Ward said, "Mr. Panadero is ready to supply what you need. We have a large amount of product already in the city, ready to distribute, as soon as we make a deal."

Ludavico smiled. "Great. Shall we keep the same terms as we had with the previous supplier?"

"Refresh my memory. What were the terms?"

"Sixty-forty split."

"We'll do seventy-thirty."

"Whoa."

"What's the problem?"

"I mean, we'll still make out on volume, but we're not prepared to take a cut."

"How long has your family had control of narcotics in New York and the East Coast?"

"Well—"

"You want to keep control, correct? Because I have three other syndicates lined up. Somebody's going to take seventy-thirty; it might as well be you."

Ludavico's featured hardened. He turned to Osborne. "Get the spreadsheets."

Gunner Osborne nodded and left the table. He was gone a few minutes; in which time nobody spoke. Ludavico kept his hostile eyes on Ward. Ward stared back. This was a poker game. He wasn't going to blink or bluff.

When Osborne returned, he carried a stack of printed pages. He handed them to Ludavico, who rotated them to show Ward. Dollar amounts lined the first page.

"I know Mr. Panadero wants a prosperous arrangement," Ludavico said. "At sixty-forty, he'll make billions. Take a look. These figures show how much we've brought in over the last six months, up until the Sevilla chain stopped. We won't talk about that."

Ward took the spreadsheets and ignored Ludavico's smile. He examined the first three pages, noting income, expenses, and net profit. Ludavico wasn't wrong. However, Ward had strict orders. He couldn't budge. He set the sheets down and explained.

"Mr. Panadero wants to make a deal today," Ward said. "I don't have the authority to negotiate, and if I go back to him with anything less, he won't be happy. Do you see my problem?"

"Do you see mine? I have my old man to answer to."

"How can we help each other?"

"Sixty-forty."

"Seventy-thirty."

Ludavico laughed. "We're not going to get anywhere."

"Call your father."

"Call your boss."

Ward smiled and held up empty hands. "I've told you my position."

Gunner Osborne grunted.

Ludavico turned to his partner. They seemed to communicate without speaking. Ludavico excused himself and walked behind Ward, passing a little too close. Ward ignored the attempted intimidation. He sipped his martini. It was good and cold. He swallowed more. He for sure needed the drink.

Osborne said, "You should see the acts we get here. Only the best. We fill that stage with a band, clear out some tables, and people dance all night."

"I'm sure it's nice."

"It's the best," Osborne said. He smiled. "I sit all night and listen. Can't beat it. You like jazz?"

"Not particularly."

Osborne frowned and stopped talking.

Ludavico returned and slid into the seat. "All right. My father isn't happy, but he agrees. We'll do seventy-thirty, but we want an option to renegotiate after six months. Can do?"

"I can ask."

"Fair enough. Will we be dealing with you in the future, or somebody else?"

"It will be me. Unless things change."

"Right. You never know, right?"

Ludavico held out his hand. Ward took it.

Connection established. Panadero had his pipeline to the East Coast. He'd deliver the news and Panadero would order the release of the stockpiled drug supply. One step closer to conquering the drug trade entirely...

38

SAÚL ELVIRA WANTED TO LOOK HIS BEST FOR WHEN THE DEA arrived.

He had never intended to play such a major role in bringing down Antonio Panadero, but it was the right move. Panadero held a sword over his head. Elvira finally had a way to take the sword out of his hand and toss it away.

Of course, the sword was his own fault. Like Panadero, he was greedy. Unlike Panadero, instead of drugs, he ripped off his clients. Elvira was an accountant in-demand in Bogota. His clients were some of the best and brightest business minds his country produced. They had so much money, Elvira didn't think they'd miss some of it. A little here, a little there. Saúl Elvira soon found himself with a huge nest egg, and managed to hide the skimming with creative math.

But then Panadero somehow found out.

How Panadero found out remained a mystery, and one Elvira never expected to solve. Panadero knew. He presented Elvira with the facts. *You're a thief; I caught you; now you will work for me and I'll pay you by not telling your clients or the cops.* From that day, the skimming stopped. Elvira wasn't taking any more risks with Panadero breathing down his neck. He did the drug baron's books, helped launder the money through various fronts, and knew every account number. He knew every individual in the Colombian government receiving a check from Panadero's front company. They were paid to look the other way, keep the police and military off his back. He had his own second set of books notating all such details; he'd bring the second set of books with him to the DEA.

He shaved carefully, not avoiding his eyes in the mirror. He felt no shame. He was doing what he needed to be free of Panadero's grasp. In the end, he'd walk away; the drug baron would rot. Or die. Saúl Elvira preferred the second option.

A dark suit waited on the bed. White shirt, black tie. Polished shoes. He was going in looking like a million bucks. When you look good, you feel good. Elvira wanted to feel good despite the butterflies in the pit of his gut. But he didn't mind them. They were normal, expected. He was walking into uncharted territory. Anybody would feel nervous.

Lastly, he grabbed a tote bag. It contained a change of clothes, personal items, and the books. The DEA promised to provide everything else he needed. He didn't need much. They promised him a new life in the United States. Witness protection. New name. New everything. He was leaving Bogota behind for good.

And he had plans for his new life. With his skills, he could start a new accounting business. He wanted to live in California's Silicon Valley, and offer his services to tech companies and their assorted workers. There was big money in tech; he knew from Bogota's own burgeoning tech sector. Easy money. He'd be set for life.

As long as he never revealed his past. As long as the cartel never caught up with him.

But if the DEA did their job right, Panadero wouldn't be around long enough to think about him ever again.

TWO FOUR-DOOR SEDANS stopped curbside in front of Saúl Elvira home. Two people exited the first. A man and a woman. Both wore sunglasses. Nobody left the second car.

Mateo Ferreria, Panadero's chief goon, watched through binoculars. He sat in his own car parked down the street. "Hello, DEA," he muttered. The man and woman walked to the front door. How many gunners waited in the second car? Elvira was getting the full escort to the police headquarters building where the US DEA shared offices with Colombian authorities.

Mateo radioed his team. They'd spread through the neighborhood in other vehicles, waiting for word. "They're picking him up. Stand by."

Mateo set the radio down and peered through the binoculars again. The second car remained motionless. The side windows showed dark tint, but he counted two men in the front seat through the clear windscreen. He turned his attention back to the front door. It opened. The man and woman emerged first, followed by Elvira. The trio walked to the first car. Elvira climbed into the back. Both vehicles executed a sharp U-turn and went the way they'd come. The back-up car followed close behind the first.

Mateo picked up the radio again. "On the move." He set down the transmitter and started his car. Tossing the binoculars on the passenger seat, he followed after them. He had a team of four working with him. They'd alternate tracking the DEA cars to avoid detection. It was a trick they'd used countless times.

His trackers weren't the only ones working this afternoon.

Mateo Ferreria had two waves of attack forces on stand-by. One would fly in via helicopters; the others by truck. Panadero's orders were clear. *Hit them hard. Make them bleed. Kill the accountant or I'll kill you for failing.*

Mateo Ferreria had no intention of letting his boss down.

———————————

RAVEN HAD to admit the holding cells were nice.

But they weren't comfortable.

Upon his arrival, Chandler and Patel once again escorted him to the basement. But instead of an interview room, they took him to a holding cell at the other end of the hall. The cell had a door with a window instead of open bars, but the accommodations within were as spartan as any jail. Wall-mounted bed, toilet, bare walls. Hollie Chandler told him the holding area was where they kept high-value informants.

"What does that make me?" Raven wanted to know.

"A temporary visitor. You're going home on the first flight tomorrow morning."

"You're not going to consider my point of view, are you?"

"No, Raven, I'm not." And she shut the cell door and grinned as she turned the lock.

He sat on the bed against the wall and enjoyed the silence. No sounds from elsewhere broke through. He sat with his thoughts and admired the sloppy paintwork on the walls. They'd slapped the stuff on instead of giving it an even spread. Blotches here and there marked the sloppiness. It gave the cell character.

He hadn't seen much of the basement area. Long hallway, maybe offices around a corner he hadn't caught a glimpse of. They'd entered via elevator, but an Exit sign hung near the interview room. He assumed there was a second door leading outside to the main grounds.

The headquarters compound impressed him. A smaller building on the street served as the point for public interaction with the local cops. Behind the perimeter wall sat the main headquarters. Large parking lot, open courtyard with palm trees, motor pool in the back. The building itself was plain, and no signs advertised what happened within. Cops in green uniforms wandered around. They were at least armed with automatic rifles and looked like they knew how to use them. But Raven didn't know how large a force covered the building. He figured they had enough in case of a cartel attack.

But the idea of an attack didn't feel realistic. The cartels had any number of ways to target police. Hitting the headquarters building wasn't one of them.

But he'd been wrong before.

He frowned as Patel and Chandler crossed in front of his cell. They didn't look through the window. They had another man with them, a fellow in a dark suit. He carried a tote bag. A few minutes later, the pair passed by minus the other man. The accountant had arrived. A high-value informant, indeed.

Raven clenched his jaw. If they thought getting him out of the country was going to change anything, they were wrong. He'd find another way back. And finish what he started.

..

39

THE TWO COMBAT CHOPPERS FLEW HIGH IN THE BLUE SKY. Busy Bogota stretched out below them. There were many tall buildings below, sunlight reflecting off steel and glass. Their destination was one building in particular, standing out in a neighborhood of smaller buildings, the Colombian flag flying atop the roof.

Six armed men rode in the cabin of each chopper. They wore heavy camouflage uniforms. Combat cosmetics streaked their hard faces. Each man carried an automatic rifle or machine gun along with a sidearm and grenades. And they had orders to lay waste to everything in their path. Distract the cops while the ground crew performed an execution in the depths of the building.

They were sending a message to the heart of Bogota law enforcement. And each man was ready to die to complete the mission.

The pilot of the lead chopper was a man named Elias Palau. Veteran of the Colombian Army, he'd been flying helicopters for as long as he could remember. He'd learned from his father, soloing at sixteen years of age. In the army, they'd taught him flying tricks his father only dreamed about. He flew for the cartels because the money was good, because there wasn't enough work for civilian pilots. It was a common story in Colombia. Nobody turned to the drug trade because they wanted to. They turned to the drug trade in desperation. To survive.

Palau had an arsenal at his fingertips. Side-mounted machine guns and rockets. He'd seen to the loading of the guns and missiles himself. All was ready. Safety covers concealed the firing switches for now, but when the fight started, he'd let 'em rip. His job was to drop the troops in the courtyard, then provide air cover during the assault. When the ground force accomplished the mission, he'd land and collect survivors. He knew he'd have fewer passengers in the end; they all knew. The trick was to make sure he was among them.

Five minutes out. He had the building in sight, and scanned his instruments and controls as he steered toward the goal. The sun beat hot through the Plexiglass cabin window. Fresh air blew inside through the port and starboard windows. His sunglasses eliminated the glare.

He wasn't a killer by nature, had never envisioned he'd take part in such an attack. But working for the cartels changed whoever set foot in their world. Once the change took place, there was no going back. Palau knew he wasn't the man he once was. He didn't like who he was now. But he had a job to do and a master to serve and there were consequences for failure.

He didn't want to fail.

Three minutes out.

MATEO FERRERIA JOINED the ground force two blocks away. He left his car and ran to the truck. Six men waited in the open bed, armed and ready. One of them handed him his gear and he suited up. Bulletproof vest. Kalashnikov AK-103. Spare mags and grenades. He didn't want a sidearm. The extra weight of a pistol would only slow him down.

The driver called to him. Mateo went to the window. Choppers beginning their final descent. The airborne attack was moments away. Mateo told the driver to start the engine and get ready. They had a short block and a half to travel before they met the perimeter wall. Then Hell would fall on police headquarters and they didn't stand a chance of stopping the attack.

Mateo knew the defensive capability backwards and forwards. Ten armed cops covered the entire building. They only had access to small arms. No heavy weapons or explosives. Building personnel weren't combat-ready. They might find weapons to shoot back with, but they were desk cops, paper pushers. Administrators and bureaucrats. Trained fighters made up Mateo's force. The cops would need to call the army for help, and the army wouldn't arrive in time. Mateo had sixteen men in the choppers and six more in the truck. More than enough.

The first crackles of automatic gunfire echoed through the afternoon. The attack had begun. Mateo jumped into the back of the truck. The driver sped off.

Mateo grinned with anticipation.

PALAU RADIOED the second chopper and said he was beginning his attack. The second chopper broke left in a sweeping turn to port. Palau turned to starboard as he cleared the parking lot. He flipped up the safety cover of the mounted machine trigger on his stick. Cutting to port, he pressed the trigger. The chopper shook as the twin cannons spit flame. The upper two levels of the building took the impact. Still drifting to port, the chopper showered the building with a stream of .50-cal projectiles. Glass shattered, the outside wall sprouting holes. Palau saw glimpses of falling bodies and screaming faces. He let up on the trigger and swept clear of the structure. A full run over the parking lot brought him and his troops back where they started. The second chopper touched down during the barrage. The first eight cartel troopers rushed across the parking lot.

Palau hovered and waited for the second chopper to lift off again. Then he set down. His men left the cabin in a rush. The second chopper fired a handful of rockets into the head-quarters building. Explosive flame erupted from the mid-level. Palau caught movement off to the right; uniformed cops with handguns fired at the troops. They were in the open, no cover; Palau lifted off and spun the chopper to face them. He fired a burst from the port-side .50-cal. The cops scattered as the steel-core slugs passed overhead. Palau pulled up and circled around again.

MATEO STOOD as the truck slowed. One of his men fired a LAW rocket from his right shoulder. The missile hit the perimeter wall. The solid concrete exploded as the high-explosive rocket dumped its energy. As flame plumed skyward, the driver stopped inches away. Mateo yelled for the other men to follow him. He took the lead, leaping off the truck and running through the hole.

Mateo moved right and took a knee as his men entered the compound. They spread out in a line. The courtyard ahead ended at one side of the building, with the motor pool behind the structure. The parked vehicles consisted of sedans, SUVs, armored transports. Mateo wanted to torch them all; there wasn't time.

An alarm blared. The fighting was at the front of the headquarters. The helicopter assault teams focused on the front, drawing resistance away from the holding cells. Mateo waved his men forward. They raced across the concrete as gunfire raged. None of the salvos came their way. They had a clear path to the side entrance leading to the underground holding cells. Mateo's primary target. The accountant Elvira had minutes left to breathe good air. Then he'd be sucking on worm fumes.

PANDEMONIUM GRIPPED THE HEADQUARTERS STAFF. Those who could, found places to hide. Those with firearms knowledge and the urge to fight back followed offices into the arms room. The officers issued automatic rifles at a hurried pace. Another officer supplied loaded magazines. The staffers loaded their weapons and stuffed spares into any available pocket. Then they ran out of the arms room to meet the incoming threat.

IN HIS HOLDING CELL, Raven heard the alarm, and pounded on the door. Had he not heard the gunfire, he'd have assumed there was a fire in progress. But the shooting meant only one thing. Attack in progress. The cartel striking to kill the accountant in the neighboring cell. The scenario he'd ruled out was coming true.

He pounded on the door some more, and tried to see

along the hall. The limited view through the window didn't allow him to see if anybody was coming to let him out.

IN THE OFFICE section of the underground holding area, elevator doors rumbled open. Bradley Patel and Hollie Chandler ran out. The desks were empty, those stationed in the basement having rushed up to aid in the fight. But the DEA agents needed to get their informant out.

"You get Elvira, I'll get Raven," Patel said as they raced through the desk area. He carried a tote bag full of weapons. The pair had joined the raid on the arms room.

"Copy," Hollie said. They ran down a short hall to the cells, turned left. Patel stopped at Raven's cell, the tall American framed in the door window. He punched the lock code and the door sprung open. Hollie entered the code to open Elvira's door.

"What's happening?" Raven said as Patel rushed into the cell. The DEA man set the tote bag on Raven's bed, pulled the zipper, and handed Raven an M-16A4 rifle. A bandoleer of six full 30-round magazines followed. Raven threw his arms through the bandoleer and slung it across his chest. He checked the rifle; round chambered, safety up, ready.

Patel gave him the rundown. The description matched Raven's assumption.

"You got a plan?" Raven said.

Patel slung his own bandoleer and racked the charging handle on his M-16. Hollie entered with the accountant. Elvira's face had gone white. He trembled, and had to lean against the wall.

Hollie answered Raven's question. "We need to get Elvira out of here."

"How many?"

"All of them for all we know," Patel said. "They're attacking at the front. We have cops and staff fighting back."

"Trained fighters?"

"No," Hollie said. "Staffers. They're going to get creamed if we don't get help."

"Has anybody called for backup?"

"Not us," Patel said. He handed Hollie her weapon and mags.

"Where are we going?" Raven asked.

"Down the hall," Hollie said. "There's a stairway. It leads to an outside access door. From there we can go around the back of the building to the motor pool and get a vehicle."

"All right," Raven said. He gripped the M-16 tight. "Show me the way."

Patel handed out the last items from the tote bag. Grenades. Raven hooked two onto his bandoleer. Hollie took two. Patel took the last pair. Elvira watched with nervous eyes. He didn't speak. He was still shaking, with a sheen of sweat now coating his forehead.

Hollie said to him, "We're going out. Stay calm. We'll protect you."

The accountant tried to nod. He opened his mouth to speak, but only a squeak came out.

Hollie took the lead. Raven and Elvira were in the middle, with Patel at the rear. They left the cell and turned right. Hollie trotted along the hall toward the other side. Raven spotted the Exit sign at the end of the hall.

———

MATEO and his men reached the outside door. The bandana around his head kept sweat from his eyes; the cloth was damp against his forehead. Mateo gestured for his explosives man. The trooper came forward, handed Mateo his rifle, and removed a heavy pack from his back. Kneeling before the door, the trooper opened the pack and took out a block of C4. He applied the block to the door. Inserting a detonator, and setting a timer, he yelled for everybody to get back. The force hustled around the corner to the motor pool. Mateo handed back the trooper's rifle. Then the explosion shook the ground. They ran around the corner again. Black smoke hung in the air; the metal door, bent and twisted off the frame, lay open a few inches. Mateo pulled it open all the way and yelled for his men to go down the steps.

Two troopers ran through the doorway. The others followed. Mateo ran in last. They started down a short flight to a hallway going left. An Exit sign hung from the ceiling. As the first of his men touched the hallway floor, automatic weapons crackled. The first two troopers screamed and jerked as bullets hammered into them. Mateo yelled for the others to stop and back up.

But he grinned, too. The other side was going to put up a strong fight after all.

40

STAFF SERGEANT VICTOR VILLA OF THE COLOMBIAN National Police was no stranger to combat. He led the defense against the incoming cartel invaders.

The lobby of the headquarters building resembled a large bank. On one side, open desks with dividers; across the tiled floor stood a long counter with more desks on the other side. A bank of elevators led to the executive offices on the upper floors.

The glass entry doors, protected from vehicular attack by large cement posts, shattered into pieces at the first barrage. Broken pieces lay across the floor. Defenders hid behind desks or the dividing walls, or from behind the counter. Villa lay on the floor with the counter on his left, yelling alerts as the cartel troops made their moves. His M-16 spit brass as he fired, and he hoped the remaining glass didn't deflect his shots too much. Several cartel troops already lay dead, blood pooling around their bodies. The other kept up a steady rate of fire. The roar of gunfire bounced off the walls and made the crackles of auto fire seem louder than they were. Villa concentrated to block the noise from registering.

They'd called the army for help, but Sergeant Villa had no idea when the nearest unit would arrive. They had to hold out till then.

Villa winced as a pair of rounds smacked into the counter wall beside him. He fired back, catching a cartel trooper in the arm. The trooper spun and fell, replaced by another. Villa settled his sights and fired again. The burst punched through the trooper's chest and knocked him flat.

Two grenades rolled to a stop in front of what remained of the glass front. Villa shouted in alarm. The blast destroyed what remained of the glass. Only the metal door frames remained. The cartel troops poured into the lobby with weapons blazing.

They caught Villa in the open. He held back the trigger and the M-16 spit out the last rounds in the magazine. Then he jumped up to meet the threat head on, colliding with an onrushing trooper, smacking the wiry man across the face with the buttstock of his rifle. He leaped over the counter as rounds tracked him. A bullet punched through the counter wall and struck his left leg as he landed. He ignored the pain as he swapped magazines and rolled onto his back. Two troopers climbing over the counter had no time to react. As Villa's muzzle found them, he fired. Both troopers' chests burst open, spewing flecks of flesh and blood; they landed in a heap around him.

Villa stayed on the floor and crawled to a desk. He joined a private there, who covered him with rapid single shots. The gunfire intensified. He rolled to his feet, scanning for targets. The defenders across the lobby at the open desks fell to the rush of cartel troopers. Villa and the private opened up on the enemy, cutting a few down. Others ran the length of the lobby to the stairwell leading up.

Villa started running. The private followed. He shouted for others to come along. There was no time to see to the dead or wounded. They had to clean out the nest of vipers who'd invaded their space and bring an end to the battle before more died.

LIGHT SPILLED into the basement hallway as the outside door exploded. Raven, Hollie, Patel and Elvira stopped midway. A doorway stood between them and the last section of hallway before the exit. Raven shouted for everybody to get down. He shouldered the M-16 and put his finger on the trigger. When two cartel troopers reached the end of the steps, he fired on full-auto. The 5.56mm rounds stitched the two troopers stomach to chest and they fell. Somebody shouted for others to hold back. Raven scooted left. The partial wall of the doorway shielded him and the others from more gunfire. He dropped the empty mag from his rifle and shoved home a new one.

"How many?" Hollie shouted beside him.

"Can't tell!"

Patel and Elvira, the accountant, were on the floor opposite them. Patel told Elvira to stay low as he pulled the pin on a grenade and rolled it ahead.

The grenade exploded in front of the steps as more cartel troopers attempted to enter the hall. Screams mingled with the blast. Patel and Raven opened fire, their shots tearing through the wall and into the stairwell. More bodies tumbled to the floor. Patel reloaded while Raven covered him, Hollie tossing a second grenade. The blast filled the hall, shaking the walls. Raven's ears rang with the combined blasts. He crossed the hall to step through the doorway, the M-16 out in front of him. Sunlight still streamed through the top of the stairs. Bodies lay on the floor and on the steps. He didn't see any more coming in.

"Is there another way out?" he yelled.

"Elevators!" Patel shouted back.

"If they're working!" Hollie added.

"Move!" Raven told them. "I'll cover!"

Raven saw the others getting off the floor in his peripheral vision. He kept his eyes forward. When Hollie yelled, he backed up through the doorway, then pivoted to run after them. They charged through the office area to the elevator. Patel pressed the call button several times. He shielded Elvira with his body as they waited.

Mateo Ferreria tried to catch his breath as he leaned against the wall outside. Only he and two other troopers remained. His face twisted in rage as he pushed away, stepped through the doorway again, and started down the steps. His two men followed. They had to step around bodies, and not slip in blood, as they worked their way down. They did step in blood, and left a trail of red footprints as they reached the hallway and started forward. Whoever had opened fire on them and tossed the two grenades was no longer present. But where had they gone? They had the accountant. They had to be stopped. The accountant could not survive the day.

Through the doorway and around the corner to the offices area...

There!

Four by the elevator. Three armed with rifles. Mateo fired from the hip. Flame flashed from the muzzle of his AK-103.

41

THE LAST THING THE CARTEL TROOPS SHOULD HAVE DONE WAS make a run for the stairwell.

Sergeant Victor Villa and the defenders in the lobby picked off a few cartel fighters as they entered the stairwell, but enough slipped through to threaten those on the upper floors. Villa had to think fast, and an idea came to him right away. He radioed to anybody who heard him on the main frequency. "Enemy troops in the stairs! Somebody throw down grenades!" A man on the third floor said he'd do so. When the explosion sounded, not even the lobby was immune to the loud bang. Villa grabbed the private and two other uniformed officers. They began the climb to find what remained of the cartel force.

Bodies tumbled to a stop in front of them as they ascended the steps, but some still lived. Not for long. Villa used his pistol to dispatch those before him. They were too stunned from the grenade blast and bloody from wounds to react in time. His men added to the body count. They climbed over more bodies, checking each. Blood covered the steps. They had to make sure not to slip. Black scorch marks covered some of the walls, the after-effect of the grenade. Villa radioed he was leading two other men up the stairs and for nobody to shoot—or drop another grenade. Several acknowledgements came in reply.

Another call came over the radio. The army had arrived. More troops entered the building. First priority: search for cartel fighters, then secure the officers. On the tails of the army trucks followed two fire engines. They'd take care of the blaze. The fire burning on the upper floors raged. Black smoke drifted from the roof and stood out for miles against the blue sky.

The police officers and army personnel focused on the above-ground floors. They didn't consider the holding cells in the basement.

RAVEN GLIMPSED Mateo Ferreria as the cartel hitter aimed from the hip, with part of his body blocked by the corner of the wall. Raven shouted, "Get down!" and fired at the same time flame flashed from the AK-103. His return fire tore chunks out of the wall. The bullets plowed through to rip through Mateo and send him sprawling. The hitter struggled to rise, his hands still clutching the rifle, and Raven shot him in the head. He dropped to a knee to change magazines. Hollie fired on the other two cartel troopers; she screamed as more shots came their way. Raven slapped his new mag home and resumed shooting. Both cartel gunmen fell to the fresh barrage of 5.56mm slugs.

Hollie screamed his name. Raven turned—and bolted for the fallen Patel, who lay across Elvira's body. Patel coughed blood and tried to rise. Raven helped him off Elvira's body and set him against the wall. That's when the elevator doors finally opened. Hollie jammed the doors with a nearby chair.

Patel told Raven to check the accountant and never mind him. Raven saw the bullet holes in Patel's chest. Blood covered his shirt and lap. There was nothing they could do even with immediate medical attention. He had, perhaps, minutes remaining.

Elvira was already gone. The cartel killers scored deadly hits before Raven's bullets found them. Raven's face fell. Their goal had been to keep him alive. They still had his books, but did they matter?

Hollie knelt beside Patel and told him to hang on, but he only smiled, said, "Go home, Hollie, and slumped to the side with his eyes still open. She began to sob.

Raven left Hollie and checked the bodies of the enemy. All three lay lifeless, bleeding out, the big man catching most of Raven's attention. He looked like the leader. Raven wondered what Panadero would think when he learned he lost his men but they'd finished their mission. Getting rid of Elvira had to be their only goal, but why attack the headquarters building? Was it a show of strength, or arrogance? Did he now know the consequences?

Raven returned to the sobbing Hollie and helped her stand.

"We need to get some help," he said.

She sniffed, wiped her eyes with the back of her right hand.

"I should have listened," she said.

"What do you mean?"

"I should have left when I had the chance."

HELP ARRIVED once they went up to the lobby and found the army well in control. They both lent a hand with the wounded, and Raven helped line the dead against the lobby's left wall. Emergency crews had a supply of body bags to put them in, and he didn't envy their task. Fire crews outside sprayed the upper floors with high-pressure water jets. Gradually, the chaos took on order, albeit the order of a disaster site clean-up. Having set aside their weapons, Raven and Hollie found a place to sit outside and watch the activity. They joined other stunned survivors under the shade of a tree. The others showed the blank stares of those who'd seen great trauma, but they worked to comfort each other. Some cried, some sat stone-faced and stared. It was a chance for everyone involved to catch their breath a moment. Reactions would come later. Raven didn't envy them, either.

"This will set us back months," Hollie said, "maybe years. My God. I can't believe he did it."

Raven let her talk.

"And Panadero will only become more powerful, almost too big to stop. We failed, Raven. All our work." She put her face in her hands. "All for nothing. And I have to go home and face another failure."

"I don't understand."

She waved him off. "Family stuff. I've been blowing them off because I didn't know what to do and that's going to blow up on me like this. And Brad..." She started to cry again. Raven put an arm around her and she leaned against him. She hadn't treated him well, but it wasn't his nature to refuse compassion when somebody needed it—even when they'd shown none to him.

When she pulled away and wiped her eyes, she looked around. Raven watched, too. More emergency crews, army troops; more fire trucks and ambulances. Men yelling, loud engines. It was going to be a few more hours before the place became quiet again.

"You were right, Raven."

"About what?"

"Dammit, you know what I mean."

"Yeah, I do."

"I'm sorry I had to learn the hard way."

"Nobody could have predicted this," Raven said, gesturing around them. "Even I thought it was off the table. But Panadero doesn't think that way, does he?"

"He has a temper. He behaves irrationally when he gets mad. I guess we made him mad. And the damn irony is it works for him."

"Well, the next time you hear about him..."

"What?"

"He'll be dead."

RAVEN WAS on his own again, but his heart was with those he'd left behind. Brave fighters in an unending war like his own, but they had more than the enemy working against them. They had to fight politics, grand-standing, corruption.

He didn't have such obstacles. All he needed were weapons and transport. He knew who to see in Bogota, and he didn't reveal his destination. Like he'd told Ward in the beginning, the cartels had spies everywhere.

Two days after the battle, Raven drove into the mountains. Top of mind was hitting Antonio Panadero where he lived. And firing a bullet through his heart.

42

RESULTS OF THE HEADQUARTERS ATTACK REACHED PANADERO through channels—his spies and informants. He ignored the first two reports. They matched, but lacked hard detail. The truth was he didn't want to believe Mateo died in the fight. By the third and fourth reports, there was no way to deny the loss of a key man. He called Salvador Costa into his private office. By the time Sal arrived, Panadero had poured two single-malts. He handed one glass to Sal, and held onto the other for himself.

"To victory, and loss," Panadero said. He raised his glass and clinked with Sal's, but Costa's face showed disagreement. Panadero ignored him. For now.

The cartel boss turned and sat behind his desk, easting into the high-backed chair. Sal sat in front of the desk.

"What happened?" Costa said.

"None of our people survived, including Mateo, rest his soul."

"And Elvira?"

Panadero grinned. "He's gone." He swallowed a mouthful of scotch. "We made the point, Sal. There is nowhere I can't reach, nobody I can't touch, and no matter how hard they try, I will always be a step ahead. And I will never fail to do the unthinkable."

Costa nodded.

"You haven't touched your drink."

"I don't see anything to celebrate."

"Don't abuse your position, Sal. I'll take *some* pushback from you—"

"Don't you understand the consequences, Tony? They'll send the *army* here."

"And our spies will tell us. We'll be ready."

Costa let out a breath. Panadero finished his glass, slammed it on the desktop, and demanded Sal hand over his if he wasn't doing to drink. Costa passed him the glass.

"We have eliminated the accountant, and completed our business in the US, thanks to Ward. Nothing can stop us now. I'll be as big, or bigger, than the mountains for the first time in my life."

Costa said nothing.

"Sal." Panadero's face turned grim. "I've already lost one trusted compatriot; shall I lose two?"

"You won't lose two. I'm thinking."

"About what?"

"About how we make sure we protect what's ours."

"The estate is protected; we have plenty of troops. If not, there are always more to collect. The army *may* come, but they won't come today. They won't come next week. We have time to arrange a proper greeting for them. I expect you'll get on that, right, Sal?"

"Yes. Anything for you, my friend."

Costa rose to leave. He turned his back on Panadero. The cartel boss's eyes burned into the back of Sal's head as he left the office.

Panadero drank more scotch. *Damn the man. Damn his*

short-sightedness. He'd come around. Once he saw the fruit of their success, he'd come around. It would only be a matter of time before he admitted how wrong he was and how Panadero had been correct the entire time.

...*PROTECT WHAT'S OURS*...
Panadero didn't understand the double meaning.

Costa cared very little for protecting the *stuff* of Panadero's estate. All he was thinking about was keeping Marina and Triana out of the inevitable crossfire. Tony was too stupid to see the flaw in his thinking.

No, he wasn't stupid, Sal corrected himself. He didn't care. His wife and "daughter" meant no more to him than the scotch in the glasses. Consumed, pissed out; forgotten.

Sal wandered to the back deck and looked at the still-unused tennis court.

He had a feeling he and his old friend would never play again. Lines had been crossed; both with the government, and personally. Sal Costa tried to be a good father; he had to do something to help Triana get clear. Marina, too. There was no time to waste. The longer he started at the tennis court, the less time the women had to escape. He truly expected the army at any minute. No way the government would allow the outrageous attack in Bogota to go unanswered. The retaliation may not be planned to the last detail, but the soldiers could wing it. They had proper motivation.

Sal left the deck in search of Marina. He wanted to see her before they went to Triana.

HE FOUND her outside looking over her garden. She stood with hands on hips examining a rose bush not quite blooming. A guard stood nearby. Costa told him to leave. Marina looked at him with an unspoken question. He told her to wait. Once the guard was out of hearing range, he touched her left shoulder. "It's happening."

"Bogota?"

"Elvira is dead and the headquarters heavily damaged. Many casualties. Mateo didn't make it," he added. Marina showed no reaction. But her worried eyes didn't leave his face. "I'm afraid the army will come," he continued. "I need to get you and Triana out of here."

"Sal—"

"You can't stay."

"Not that. Tony will just tell us to go to the safe room if something happens."

"Not good enough. They'll burn this place to the ground. And I want you both out of the way."

"What about you?" she said.

"I'll stay with Tony. With any luck, we can both get away, too. But we'll be on the run."

"He won't run. You know that, Sal."

"Then I'll die knowing you and Triana are safe."

She put a hand to her mouth; tears welled in her eyes.

"Now is not the time." He pulled her close and squeezed her once. Before she hugged back, he pushed her away. "Go find our daughter. Tell her. I'll get a car ready for you both."

She threw her arms around him and squeezed tight. He hugged back. Resolve remained, but sadness filled him, too. They wouldn't see each other again. If he was right. If he was wrong, Tony's wrath would bring the same fate.

RAVEN PROWLED THE JUNGLE.

He'd come prepared for war, and carried the requisite tools. The Nighthawk Custom .45 rode on his hip. His combat vest contained six grenades and spare mags for the rifle he carried. In his hands as lead weapon, the hammer punch, the bringer of death—a mainstay of the US SEALs. The MK-14 Mod O was an "enhanced" version of the M-14 semi-automatic service rifle. With a high-powered scope and pistol grip, it was the perfect weapon with which to reach out and kill at long distance.

Dressed in camouflage with heavy-duty combat boots, Raven moved through the overgrowth. He ignored the sweat covering his body. Two canteens provided water during his infrequent breaks.

Getting into the jungle had been easy. Contacts in Bogota got him in touch with a weapons supplier, who also provided transport. The truck driver dropped Raven off ten miles from his target; Raven traveled the rest of the way on foot. Getting out? Raven decided he'd have to wing it. For now, only the mission mattered. Kill Panadero. Avenge his friends. *Every last one of them.*

And he hadn't forgotten Kendrick Ward in the United States. Assuming he survived the hit on Panadero, New Jersey was Raven's next stop. He'd end it where it began. A check-in with Clark Wilson at the CIA before heading into the jungle brought news Raven knew he'd hear. Ward had established Panadero's East Coast connection. And with the same New York syndicate Sevilla had used. If Raven didn't succeed, Panadero's drugs would flow into the United States. Thousands of lives were at risk. The DEA was out of the equation. It was up to Raven.

He dropped to one knee to listen and scan. He didn't sense any threats, but the jungle was so thick anything could hide with ease. And he wasn't a native. A potential enemy knew hiding spots he didn't. He sipped some water. It was silent, no wind; he was alone in the world. And he didn't like the feeling. Stowing the canteen, gripping the MK-14 again, he resumed his march. According to the GPS unit on his left wrist, he was two miles from the target. He had a good idea where to set up his sniper's nest.

Raven stepped over the thick brush, ducked to avoid low branches, negotiated the dips and rises. Coming to a stream, he used the rock tops jutting out of the water to hop across. Then he stopped to top off one canteen and drop a purification tablet down the neck. He continued. The bandanna around his head kept sweat from dripping into his eyes, but the band felt soaked. Soon, he'd have to change to a dry one.

He kept moving. Not long now.

43

RAVEN STRETCHED OUT ON THE GROUND AND POKED THE sniper rifle between the trunks of two trees. Leaves covered him; his camouflage provided the rest of the concealment. The bipod under the rifle's hand guard folded down without noise, and he set the legs in the ground. Peering through the scope, he examined Panadero's estate. The compound lay half a mile away.

The scope showed him a portion of the rear of the house. Especially the back balcony, and part of the wrap-around walkway. The heads and shoulders of guards patrolling the walkway made for attractive targets. But Raven focused on the balcony. Panadero had to step out sometime. When he did...

A rustle behind him.

By the time he turned, four men and a woman had guns pointed at him. The woman held his attention, but not because of her striking appearance. He recognized her face.

He was less than a foot away from Yasmina Sevilla.

The daughter of Martin Sevilla.

The man Kendrick Ward hired Raven to kill.

The four men fanned out behind Yasmina. In their camo and face paint, only their sharp eyes stood out. But they were all wiry, with the look of seasoned hunters, and they knew how to handle their M-16 rifles.

Yasmina wore her uniform sinched at the waist by a pistol belt. The holster didn't contain a sissy gun. Raven recognized the rubber grips of a Taurus Model 44. And she likely had the six cylinders stoked with full power magnum loads. The gun she held on him now was a battered MP5.

"Hello, Yasmina," Raven said.

"You know me, but I don't know you." She spoke English with a light accent.

"Depends on your plans."

"And what do you think my plans are?"

"With all these guns, looks like you're about to shoot me."

"Not without knowing your name first. I never kill a man I don't know the name of."

"You keep a scrap book?"

"Be careful I don't make an exception in your case."

Raven believed she might.

MARINA FOLLOWED the sounds of the piano. She found her daughter testing note combinations, playing at random to see what fit. Marina hated to interrupt, but she had to. She entered the room and came up behind Triana. The younger woman didn't hear her approach. She gasped when her mother touched her shoulders and turned her head.

"You startled me!"

Marina told her to scoot over. She joined her daughter on the bench. Triana noticed the grim set to her jaw because she looked alarmed.

"Keep playing."

"Mom, what's—"

"Keep playing and listen."

Triana's hands glided across the keys. She wasn't experimenting any longer. The tune was a well-practiced one. Marina leaned close.

"We have to go. Tony—your *father* has made some bad choices and Uncle Sal wants us to go."

"What?" Triana continued playing without a hiccup.

"Come on, let's go up to your room and pack."

"But—"

"Don't argue. *Now*."

Triana lifted her hands from the keys as if they had turned red hot.

When they reached Triana's bedroom, her mother shut the door and grabbed a suitcase from the closet.

"Mom, we talked about this. Daddy won't—"

"Sal will protect us. He's getting a car ready."

"But why does Uncle Sal—"

Marina took Triana by the shoulders again.

"Listen to me very carefully. This will be hard to hear. But Sal is your *real* father."

Marina watched the color drain from Triana's face. Her mouth dropped open in shock.

"Sal and I had an affair, and we hid it from Tony. Sal loves you move than anything, and wants us safe. Now, help me pack for you."

Marina moved to the dresser. She opened the drawers and began gathering clothes.

But Triana stood still. Her mother's words hit like a punch in the gut. Her pulse quickened and her knees wobbled. She sat on the bed and stared at the carpet. Her mother moved fast, stuffing the suitcase, but Triana's mind spun with questions.

"Triana, *help* me. We have to hurry."

Triana stood and went to the walk-in closet. She gathered clothes but moved in slow motion. At least it seemed like she moved in slow motion. Her thoughts became scrambled. Panic set it. She breathed fast. Images from the past flooded her mind.

She didn't see "Uncle" Sal with her; she saw him with her mother. The whispered conversations; the way he touched her when opportunity allowed; the looks they sometimes shared. What she'd dismissed as the intimacy of lifelong friends took on a new meaning in light of her mother's bombshell.

Then she got mad.

"Why did you lie to me?" Triana threw the clothes at the suitcase as her mother set another bundle within. Her mother spun to face her.

"You know Tony. You know him too well."

"How *could* you!" Triana's vision flooded. She didn't wipe her eyes.

"It wasn't something we meant to happen. It just happened."

Triana sobbed.

Marina grabbed her in a tight hug. Despite her feelings, Triana clutched at her mother, too.

Her life had been a lie and she wanted to lash out. She wanted the truth. But truth held her in a close embrace. How could she be angry at her mother? She not only indeed knew the man she'd believed was her father, but also knew her mother was the more caring of the two. And Sal. "Uncle" Sal. He'd always been present when her "father" chose to be distant. Another clue. Her mother wasn't lying. She and Sal hid their affair to save their lives.

And hers.

"Okay." Triana pulled away. "All right," she said.

"I'm sorry. I'll explain everything once we get out of here."

"Where are we going?"

"I don't know. We'll find somewhere."

They resumed packing as a team.

———

RAVEN SAID, "My name is Sam Raven."

Yasmina Sevilla's face showed no reaction.

"Hello, Mr. Raven. You're American?"

"Yes."

"Did the CIA send you?

"No. I'm here on my own."

"Why?"

Raven kept his poker face straight. It took work to ignore the muzzles trained on him. He couldn't afford to tell her the real story, so he gave her a new version—one *close* to reality.

"I'm here to kill Panadero because he murdered five friends of mine. He hired them under false pretenses. When they finished the job—"

"He killed them in a helicopter attack."

Raven frowned. *How much does she know?* "Yes," he said.

"Do you know what he hired them to do?"

Raven nodded. "Kill your father."

"Yes, those men *murdered* my father."

"Then you understand—"

Her right hand flashed to the gun on her hip. She pressed the muzzle of the stainless .44 to his head. The hammer clicked back as she brushed her thumb over the spur. Raven kept his breathing steady. The big slugs visible in the chambers would bring an end to his crusade in the blink of an eye.

"You don't get to kill Panadero, Mr. Raven. Only I get to. Understand?"

"Yes, ma'am," Raven said.

Yasmina smiled. She lowered the hammer while still pointing the gun, then returned it to its holster. At the snap of an order, her men lowered the M-16s.

Raven allowed himself a relaxing sigh.

"I know enough of the story," she told him. "Enough to know you aren't lying."

"Do you want me to leave?"

"Are you kidding?"

"I'd like to know what you're thinking, Yasmina. We're here for the same purpose. There's no reason for *us* to be enemies."

"You may join my attack force, but you answer to me."

Raven considered her words. If he agreed too fast—

"I think I'll leave it to you," he said.

"Mr. Raven." Her hand moved to the revolver again. "Don't make me change my mind."

"What do you have planned?"

"My people are setting up to attack," she said. "I have snipers, but another is not a bad idea. You will provide covering fire for my people. Shoot as many of Panadero's goons as you want, but the big prize is mine."

"I understand."

Yasmina addressed one of her men, a burly fellow; Raven caught his name. Michael. She told him to stay and cover "Mr. Raven" until he heard from her over the radio. Raven pretended not to understand the exchange. Michael agreed, and nodded at Raven. Raven nodded back. Yasmina explained she was leaving Michael with him, and Raven didn't argue. He shook hands with the fellow awkwardly.

"Be seeing you," Yasmina said. She directed her remaining teammates away from the sniper nest.

Raven looked at his watcher. "English?"

Michael shook his head.

"We'll just grunt then." Raven smiled. So did Michael. Raven wasn't sure what the fellow thought he understood, but it was a start.

44

YASMINA SCOWLED AS SHE AND HER MEN CUT THROUGH THE jungle like they'd been born there. They had. Slicing through the dense growth was as natural to her as breathing. The heat didn't bother her. The bugs didn't concern her. She was in her element, and about to deliver final justice to the man who ripped her world apart.

The son of a bitch Raven. She knew he was lying. She knew he'd been with the mercenaries he called his friends. Her investigation into what happened had been thorough. There were six mercenaries, not five, and rumors of a survivor. All she knew was Panadero's people counted five bodies. But her sources told her he hired six men for the job. Raven must have been the survivor.

A smart woman would know the hired guns weren't truly responsible for her father's death. Panadero was. Kendrick Ward was the other. But Yasmina didn't care. She was her father's daughter, and revenge had to be swift, brutal, and uncompromising. She'd deal with Raven once her primary goal no longer existed. Then a trip to New Jersey sounded nice...

She had time to focus on revenge now that she'd gained control of her father's operations. The battle for supremacy cost a lot, but she'd come out the victor. After she took care of Ward, she'd reestablish her father's—and now *her*—dominance in the drug trade. Conflicts might interrupt business, but business never stopped for long. Business always continued no matter what. Too many people needed their drugs to get through each day.

Her forces massed on the east side. They'd blow the wall and run into the compound. Yasmina's orders were clear. *Nobody survives. Kill them all.*

The drug world would quickly learn Yasmina Sevilla was very much her father's duplicate.

Presently, she and her crew met the rest of the attack force. The eastern wall of Panadero's property lay ahead. They'd have to run across open grass to reach the main building. She had to reach Panadero before he reached the hardened safe room in the basement. But if he did get inside, one of her men had a particular explosive handy to make the door of the vault-like room melt away. But she didn't think she'd need the device. She expected Panadero to fight with the rest of his gunmen.

She eased to the front line. Two of her crew carried LAW rocket launchers, the tubes extended and primed. She gave them the go ahead and checked her MP5 one last time. She'd brought the Taurus .44 Magnum to use on Antonio Panadero. One shot, one kill. She'd have liked to feed him to her pet alligators at her own estate, but playing games caused mistakes. She didn't want him getting away, somehow, because she fooled around. A .44 to the face would do the job.

The pair with the LAW launchers fired at the same time. A boom and flash of back blast; the rockets hit the wall at the speed of a lightning flash. Yasmina turned away prior to the explosion. She looked back to see a ball of flame consuming the stone wall, the cloud trailing skyward, a big gap where the wall had been. Yasmina didn't need to shout the order to attack. Her team rushed through, climbing over the pile of debris. The crackles of M-16s filled the air. Yasmina ran through with the rest of her force behind her.

The well-tended lawn Panadero must have been proud of became a battle ground.

Yasmina charged across the open field. As return fire came from the house, she zigzagged, dropped and rolled; any move to confuse the aim of defenders. The bullets whistled overhead at a furious rate. Her men duplicated her moves, but they also fired back.

Behind her, at the gap in the wall, the two men who'd blasted the way through aimed another pair of LAW rocket tubes. The launchers thumped their messages of destruction. Finned high-explosive projectiles smashed into the house. One blast destroyed a portion of the second-level walkway. And the two Panadero troops firing from it. The debris rained down the side of the house, smashing first-floor windows, and crushed a trio of defenders rounding the corner.

The second rocket hit the uppermost floor. The fireball flared for a moment, and ignited the roof. The flames began to spread across the roofing tiles.

The Panadero troops were slow responding. By the time the defenders reached the side under attack, they faced the full force of the Sevilla assault. Yasmina and her men gained the wide patio and spread out. Automatic weapons fire blazed; men clashed hand-to-hand; others fell to salvos of lead.

And watching it all through his sniper scope was Raven. He picked off Panadero troops as he found them. The MK-14 kicked hard with each shot, but each round found its mark and added to the body count. Burning through the ten-round magazine, he loaded another with haste, and resumed his gaze through the scope. He watched as Yasmina led a small group around to the front. They disappeared around the corner of the house. *On your own, hon.* Others focused on the rear. Raven turned his attention to the second contingent.

The flames atop the roof burned and spread further. Black smoke drifted in waves toward the sky.

Raven tilted the muzzle up to scan the walkway and rear windows. No threats lurked on the walkway. But he paused at a window in the back wall not connected to the wrap-around path. The face of a young woman, frightened, appeared behind the glass.

Raven's mental mug file provided her identity. Triana Panadero, the boss's daughter. A pair of hands connected to somebody Raven didn't see pulled her away.

Great, Raven thought. *Non-combatants in the mix.*

Raven brought the muzzle down. He began tracking targets again as the rear force prepared to break through the back of the house.

WHEN THE EXPLOSION SOUNDED, Triana and her mother froze mid-move. They exchanged worried looks, and then the gunfire started. They heard men yelling, running; louder gunfire as troops opened up from the walkway.

"Sal was right," Marina said.

Triana ran to the window and pulled the curtains aside. She watched the flow of attackers running across the grass. The house shook from additional impacts. Marina yelled for Triana to get back, but the girl couldn't pull her eyes away. *Someday* had become reality. She worried the strength she'd mentally awarded the man she'd thought of as her father wouldn't save him after all. It wouldn't save her mother or her if they didn't get away. But how could they escape in the middle of a battle?

Her mother grabbed her and pulled her back. No words were necessary. They hurried to zip the two suitcases—Triana has insisted on a second—and then the door flew open. Sal Costa stepped through. He left the door partway open.

"Is it the army?" Marina asked.

"No, somebody else," Sal said.

"Who?" Triana asked.

"I have a car ready," Sal said. He handed Triana a set of car keys. She took them. "If we—"

Triana threw her arms around him. He stumbled, uncertain. Marina said, "I told her," and he finally hugged back.

"I wish it wasn't like this," Sal said.

"It's okay," Triana told him.

The door opened all the way. Panadero held the door with one hand and a gun in the other.

"What are you waiting for? You should be in the safe room." He noticed the suitcases on Triana's bed. "What's this?"

"We're leaving!" Triana shouted.

"It's too late to leave. Come on. We're going to the basement." He used his free hand to grab her and began to drag her out despite resistance.

She shouted, "No!" and stomped on one of his feet. Panadero jumped back, startled, and let go. His angry glare set Triana off.

"You're not my father!"

"Dammit, child," he snapped. His free hand moved in a flash. The back of his hand struck her in the jaw and she cried out as she fell to the floor.

Her mother tried to move toward her, but her legs

wouldn't move. She was shaking as she waited for the next moment.

Sal said, "Tony. She's telling you the truth."

"Are you crazy? We're under attack!" The gunfire continued outside. The attacking force had not yet entered the house.

But Sal's eyes bored into Panadero's. The cartel boss examined his old friend's face. A scowl formed. Panadero understood. Sal wasn't crazy. And he wasn't lying.

"She's mine," Sal said.

Marina realized Sal didn't have a gun.

But she willed herself to move. She stepped closer to Sal, blocking her sobbing daughter from Panadero's gaze. Triana still lay on the carpet.

Panadero's face turned red. "Are you...Did you..."

"It's true," Marina said.

Panadero's vision tunneled on them both. The people closest to him, as a range of images from the past flooded his mind. He'd seen the looks, the moments, the interactions easy to dismiss because Sal had been part of his life for so long. Now, those moments took on new meaning. They'd betrayed him. They'd mocked him in their presence, behind his back; the young woman he thought was the best of him wasn't part of him at all.

Panadero raised his gun.

45

AND SHOT SAL IN THE FACE.

As Costa's body fell back onto the bedspread, Marina watched him fall. She pivoted sharply to face Panadero again, hands out in front of her. She screamed. Nothing coherent escaped her lips; it was a cry of sheer terror as her husband turned his gun on her.

He fired three times. The third bullet missed as Marina was already crumpling to the floor. She landed inches from where her daughter lay. Triana watched her mother die through tear-filled eyes. Her own scream drowned out the ringing of the gunfire.

Triana bolted to her feet. Panadero stood dumbfounded, seemingly unaware of the gun he held. She felt the keys her true father had given her digging into her left palm. She ran past Panadero, out the door, and began a desperate sprint down the long hallway.

She didn't look back. But she heard Panadero yelling her name. She heard the shot he fired. The bullet didn't connect. It zipped overhead to smack into the wall ahead. She reached the corner, spun right, and raced down a set of steps. If she hurried, hurried like her mother wanted, she still had a chance to get away...

A GRENADE TOOK down the double doors.

The explosion filled the porch, blasting debris down the steps to the stone walkway out front. Yasmina urged her men forward. They stepped over the bodies of Panadero troops as they finally entered the house. Her MP5 spit flame. She and her team engaged troops waiting inside. The flurry of rounds ripped apart the walls, paintings, any standing decoration. A hallway crossed left-to-right ahead, and Yasmina spotted the staircase there, too. As she headed for the hall, a girl ran down the stairs and turned right down the hallway. By the time Yasmina reached the same point, the girl was gone. She told her men to follow her. They started up the steps. She let the MP5 dangle on its sling and filled her right hand with the Taurus .44 Magnum. She was close to the prize. She felt Panadero near.

PANADERO GATHERED himself as he watched Triana run down the stairs. There was no time to think. He had to act. He still had his empire; he'd find another wife. There were always women around. What he needed to do now was get away and regroup. As long as he remained alive, rebuilding wasn't impossible.

He started down the hall at a quick pace.

Then a blast shook the front of the house, a blast so sharp it rocked the floor. Panadero fell against the wall and to the carpet. His pistol tumbled from his hands. He crawled to the gun, grabbed it, and stood again. He paused as automatic

234 | BRIAN DRAKE

weapons fire erupted from the ground floor. As fast as it had
started, it stopped. A woman's voice shouted commands. *No!
No, it will not end here!* Panadero slapped a full magazine into
his pistol and ran for the stairs. He was three floors up, but
he'd meet the invaders head-on if it was the last thing he
ever did.

Down one flight, left turn—

He met Yasmina halfway between the second and third
floors. Their eyes met for only a second, but a moment was
all it took.

Panadero brought up his pistol. The gaping mouth of the
.44 Magnum rose faster.

———————————

YASMINA FIRED THE .44. Panadero's head snapped back. As
his body fell against the steps, his pistol discharging, she
flinched. The bullet didn't hit her. The slug tore a chunk out
of the wall beside her instead. She holstered her revolver and
gazed on the dead body with a sense of satisfaction. She'd
avenged her father; she'd take everything Panadero left
behind.

Her radio crackled as she and her crew descended back to
the ground floor. She snatched the two-way from her belt.
"Yes?"

"A woman took a car from the garage," a man reported.
"She crashed through our barricade and the main gate."

Yasmina frowned. "Was she alone?"

"Yes, ma'am."

The girl running from the stairs...

"It's Panadero's daughter," Yasmina said into the radio.
"Find me a vehicle and get it running. We're going after her."

The job wasn't done until she wiped out any last trace of
Panadero's bloodline.

RAVEN LOOKED up from his scope. The fight was over. The fire would consume the house, burn it to the ground. But the victor was clear. He turned to his babysitter, the man named Michael, and smiled. Michael smiled back. Then he hurried to answer a radio call from Yasmina. He set his M-16 down to do so. Raven sat up as the pair talked. He again pretended not to understand the exchange.

"We're clearing out," Yasmina advised. "Somebody got away—Panadero's daughter. I'm going after her. I'm leaving Jorge in charge to get you back to base. Before you go, kill the American."

"Yes, yes," Michael said. He started to pick up his rifle.

Raven snatched out the Nighthawk .45 and turned his body to face Michael. He fired once and shot the other man through the head. As Michael's body slumped over, Raven said, "Sorry, pal," then slipped the .45 back into the holster on his right hip.

He left the MK-14 and took Michael's M-16 and spare magazines. He had to stop Yasmina from killing the girl. Non-combatants were off-limits. He didn't care who the girl's father was. She wanted to get away from the fight; she deserved a chance to do so. She didn't deserve the same fate as her father.

The way in was the same way Yasmina had gone.

Raven ran for the hole in the wall...

YASMINA STOOD in the truck bed. She braced her MP5 on the roof while fighting to keep balance as the truck took curves at high speed. They'd yet to catch up with Panadero's daughter. The witnesses who saw her race off said she drove a silver Mercedes. With no other traffic on the road, how hard could it be to catch up? Unless she'd already reached the highway connection. But Yasmina didn't think she'd had enough time. What if the girl knew a side road? Something Yasmina had missed. She didn't have a map. Her crew back at the estate had maps to guide them out of the area, a route taking them away from the main highway, but she hadn't packed one for herself.

Dammit!

No, focus. Hold on. She's on this road!

Yasmina had three men with her. Two inside the cabin, one in the truck bed with her. The gunner with her leaned over the driver's side of the bed, his weapon at the ready should the Mercedes appear. The wind whipped at Yasmina's face, but she ignored it. She wanted the daughter dead at her feet like Panadero. She replayed in her mind the vision of the .44 coring his head. It made her smile.

But for her own safety, she dared not tell the driver to go faster. There was no way to enjoy revenge if you yourself were dead. And what a lousy way to go, thrown from the back of a truck during a moment of triumph.

The road curved again. She shifted with the movement. The rockface on the right prevented her from seeing around the corner. The road straightened, and she finally saw the silver Mercedes.

"There she is!" Yasmina lined up the front and rear sights of the MP5 on the back of the silver car. The straight road allowed the driver to increase speed and close the gap. She squeezed the trigger. The burst of 9mm rounds punched holes in the truck, passing through the gas tank. Fuel spilled onto the roadway. Yasmina adjusted her aim ahead of the car. She fired again, letting off the trigger before exhausting the rounds in the magazine.

Her salvo stitched holes in the roof, punctured more of

the trunk, and the left rear tire. The rubber popped, chunks flying back at the truck. Yasmina achieved what she wanted. The Mercedes spun, the front end pointing at the rockface as the car spun perpendicular. The front end clipped the rock and jolted to a sudden stop, continuing its spin. The driver's side hit the rockface, the front end pointing at the oncoming truck. The driver hit the brakes and stopped less than ten feet from the smashed silver Mercedes. Yasmina eyed the long-haired driver, who hunched behind the wheel, unmoving. She appeared uninjured.

For now.

Yasmina leaped out of the truck. The gunmen with her followed, and she told the two up front to join her, too. The four, Yasmina in the lead, walked casually toward the Mercedes. Yasmina took the time to change out the near-empty mag in the MP5 for a full one. Then she flicked the selector switch to single-shot.

Panadero's daughter watched them through the windshield. She gripped the wheel with both hands, knuckles white. Her face showed panic and uncertainty. Her big eyes widened further when she saw the automatic weapons.

Yasmina smiled. She shouldered the MP5 and aimed at the glass.

46

TRIANA HAD TO FIGHT TO BREATHE. FEAR HELD HER IN SUCH A tight grip, she couldn't think or move. She'd taken a hard jolt in the driver's seat, but the seatbelt kept her from injury. So did the side airbag which blew and cushioned the impact. As she sat shaking in the driver's seat, she watched the four people coming to kill her. Why couldn't they have let her go? She had nothing to do with her father's business.

Panic turned a sub into a scream as the woman in the lead shouldered her weapon and aimed. She told two of her men to get "the girl" out. They pulled opened the passenger door and one reached inside. Finally, Triana moved. She screamed and slapped at him, but the seatbelt held her in place. Her resistance stopped when the gunman punched her in the mouth. Stunned, she leaned against the deflated airbag. The man's big hands reached for the seatbelt buckle.

The gunman and his partner dragged her kicking and screaming over the center console. Her attempt to break away did nothing. They dropped her on the pavement. She sprawled once again, this time on the hot asphalt. It felt rough on the palms of her hands and scraped her knees through her jeans as she tried to get up. She looked up at the woman. The woman turned her gun muzzle on Triana's face. Her index finger tightened around the trigger.

Another vehicle engine revved at high speed. One of the men shouted an alarm. They all turned to face a second oncoming vehicle racing toward them.

———————

RAVEN PAUSED at the blown-out section of the wall. He couldn't wait long. Yasmina had a head start. But he also couldn't go charging across the property, until he learned what he faced.

He watched through the sights of the M-16. Yasmina's men were busy up front, and he only had a partial glimpse of the activity. But he recognized a withdrawing force when he saw one, heard the rumble of starting engines. He hoped there'd be a vehicle still available for him.

He bolted across the grass for the rear patio, slipping inside through blasted doors. Lots of dead bodies and damage as he made his way to the long hallway and headed for the garage. The Sevilla activity remained outside, but faded as the vehicles departed. Raven stepped into the garage. Panadero's personal cars. Two rows, front ends facing each other, aisle down the middle. A board hung on the wall held keys and key fobs. He grabbed a fob and began pressing the unlock button. Lights flashed on a Jeep. Raven ran to it and climbed inside. Starting the motor with the push-button start, he pulled out and turned left for the open garage doors.

But not every member of Yasmina's force had gone.

Two of her troopers raced inside at the sound of the Jeep starting. Raven aimed the front end at them and pressed the accelerator. One leaped out of the way. The other went *thump-bump* under the wheels, jolting Raven in his seat. Seconds later, he was on smooth pavement. He sped down the access road to the mountain road, making a sharp left. He sped up some more, but the first two sudden curves made him back off the throttle. He didn't want to end up smeared on the right side rockface or crash off the road in the forest.

Where had the rest of Yasmina's men gone? He hoped they took a different road. If he ran into them, Triana Panadero didn't have a chance. Passing a side road gave him the answer, a flash of the back end of the last truck in the convoy. They were going another way. Raven set his attention ahead.

He hoped he wasn't too late.

But if so, he'd see to it Yasmina Sevilla never enjoyed the fruits of her vengeance.

He kept driving with his hands tight on the wheel. All he saw was twisty blacktop.

And then...

He came around a curve and ahead lay the truck and wrecked Mercedes. He saw Yasmina standing in the street with her men and there was Triana Panadero on the ground. He stomped the brakes as gun muzzles turned his way.

He twisted the wheel and spun the Jeep sideways, passenger side facing the enemy. A tug on the emergency brakes rocked the Jeep to a final halt. Raven rolled out as the fusillade of automatic weapons fire tore into the Jeep. With the M-16 gripped close to his chest, he ran to the front fender and fired over the hood. Two quick bursts. Yasmina ran for cover. One of her men fell, and Raven sighted on another. He squeezed. The gunner staggered and dropped, landing near Triana. Raven wanted to yell for her to stay down, but didn't think she'd hear. He ran from the Jeep into the foliage off the shoulder. Gunfire tracked him, smacking into thick leaves and tree trunks. Raven ducked and dodged the natural obstacles as he ran parallel to the road. He needed to get closer to Yasmina's position. When he did, he and aimed through a gap and fired at the last gunman. The 5.56mm bullet zipped through his neck, spraying Yasmina with a burst of blood as he fell. She turned his way, bringing the MP5 with her, and Raven held his position. He fired again. Yasmina jerked as the first slug went through her belly; Raven's follow-up pushed her nose out the back of her head. Her body landed on top of the gunner, and the echo of shots faded. Only the sound of Triana's sobs filled the space.

Raven climbed the short slope, pushing branches and leaves out of his way. He ran to Triana. Aside from a bloody lip, she looked okay. But he knew she was only okay on the surface. He knew better than to ask if she was all right in general. Even well-meaning questions were sometimes the wrong ones. Triana sat up and scooted back. She touched her lip and winced.

"Who are you?" she asked him.

The guy who wanted to kill your Dad before the crazy lady showed up.

Raven said, "You looked like you needed help. I happened to be here."

"Is she dead?"

Raven nodded. "She'll only show up in your dreams. But hopefully not."

Triana hurried to her feet. Raven stood, too. She began shaking when she saw the wrecked Mercedes and the shot-up Jeep. But then her eyes changed. "Wait. That's my—that Jeep is from the garage." She glared at Raven. "Who *are* you?"

"It's a long story, Triana. But I'm here to help if you want. The truck looks okay. You can drive it still."

Triana attempted to reply, but a sudden noise interrupted the conversation. Army green helicopters, with military markings, flew overhead. A mass of them. Loaded with weapons and men, the Huey choppers sped in the direction of the Panadero estate.

"My father—my *real* father—was right. There's the army."

The swarm of helicopters continued. Raven counted at least fifteen. They finally passed over. The cacophony of rotor blades faded into the wind.

"Who's your father? I thought—"

She shook her head. "It's a long story. I'm taking the truck. Do you want a ride somewhere?"

Raven considered, but decided he shouldn't. She might ask him questions he didn't want to answer.

"Well—"

"Hey. I, uh, could use the company. I don't know what to do now."

Raven said okay. "We can go to Bogota. I have a few friends who can help you."

She tried hard not to look nervous. She started for the truck. "Tell me where to go," she said. "Or do you want to drive?"

Raven took the wheel.

Neither spoke on the ride into the city.

47

NEW JERSEY.

He'd end it where it began.

Kendrick Ward's estate sat behind an iron gate and a brick wall fronted by trees. Another "impregnable" fortress. Raven laughed. He'd found the weak spots after watching the house the first night of his arrival.

He climbed one of the trees, stepped out, and made the short jump to the top of the brick wall. He crouched. The house and yard sat in darkness, as did the other homes spread out through the neighborhood. The electric company would later discover a C-4 charge destroyed the junction box. Which also turned off Ward's security systems. The systems included light-beams across the yard to alert those inside to intruders.

But the lack of electrical power didn't turn off the human element of Ward's defenses.

They made a lot of noise, too, Raven noticed.

Ward had six men at the house. Six tough-looking brutes, five of whom stayed in the detached guest house. Zac Fox,

244 | BRIAN DRAKE

the big goon with the beard, stayed in the main house. Raven knew their routines. He'd been watching for a week.

Ward knew, by now, of Panadero's demise. If Ward trusted the official report of the army raid, he wasn't worried about Raven. Since he remained at his home, Raven decided Ward indeed believed the official report.

Raven dropped from the top of the wall to crouch on the grass. The cloudy night allowed no glare of moonlight, but he wouldn't remain concealed for long. Zac Fox and his security team carried flashlights. They swung the beams back and forth as they moved further away from the house. But not closer to Raven. The men stopped where the patio met the grass, 30 yards from the wall where Raven crouched. From their chatter, they didn't appear alarmed. The other blacked-out homes assured them the outage was not an anomaly.

Raven stretched out flat and continued to wait.

He'd come prepared. Pistol in shoulder harness, grenades clipped to a heavy-duty belt. Head weapon was an old friend, the Colt M-4 Commando, a 12-inch barreled version of the US M-4. It packed the same punch of 5.56mm NATO rounds. The barrel of Raven's M-4C was a little longer because of the attached suppressor.

Fox's men were ready to call it normal and go back to the guest house. Only Fox himself hesitated and told them to wait. Raven sighted on Fox. The big man was hard to miss in the glow of the other flashlights. But he didn't fire. He wanted to kill Fox in the name of Fireplug Starkey. He'd kill him last, if possible. Save him for dessert, so to speak. But Raven touched the M-4C's trigger anyway. *Not yet...*

Raven shifted his aim to the security men to the right of Fox. He'd seen them about during his observations. They walked around with pistols. He assumed they had access to more, but they hadn't brought more with them. He didn't know who they were and didn't care. They took orders from Fox, a man with an organized crime background; it was enough.

He fired once. The body in the flashlight glare jerked and fell. The others reacted with yells and moved as Raven expected. Two broke into a sprint for the guest house. Fox and the remaining two dug out their handguns and fired back. At random. Their shots came nowhere near him.

Raven sighted on the man beside Fox. They shuffled back to the safety of the house. Raven didn't let them get there. He triggered more single shots, firing fast, the M-4C spitting slugs. Only the clack of the weapon's action made any noise as the 5.56mm rounds covered the distance. The two men hit the patio in respective heaps. Raven let Fox run into the house. He fired two rounds over the big man's head. The bullets smacked into the wall above the patio door.

The guest house. He needed to get closer. Raven slung the M-4C and grabbed a grenade from his belt. Pulling the pin, he started running. He reached the halfway point. The two men emerged toting submachine guns. Raven threw the grenade and hit the grass. The blast ripped both men apart. Raven regripped the M-4C and closed in on the house. Another grenade blew the patio doors clear. A sea of broken glass and parts of the metal door frames landed on the cement. Raven stepped through. A light mounted on the rifle highlighted the inside. He guided around furniture, his steps silent on the soft carpet. Voices from above reached his ears. Two men arguing. A woman screaming for them to do something. Raven kept moving. Up a staircase to a hallway. Voices louder now. He continued forward. Flashlight beams danced in a room at the end of the hall. The arguing went on, Ward demanding action from Fox, Fox slamming the phone and saying it didn't work. Raven grinned. He'd cut the phone lines, too.

He reached the open doorway and swung inside. The beam of light caught Mrs. Ward and she screamed. The men stopped yelling. Raven fired twice. Fox went down. Raven shot him again, in the right arm, as the big man clawed for his gun.

Ward ran out in front of his wife with his hands up.

"No! Raven! Don't!"

Raven dropped his aim and pulled the trigger.

Ward's left knee popped like a cracked egg. He fell, his scream louder than his wife's, and writhed on the carpet. His wife, hiding behind a chair, put a hand to her mouth and called his name through her fingers.

Fox tried to reach his gun with his left hand. Raven kicked the gun away. Over the noise made by the Wards, he said, "Remember Starkey?"

Fox stared into the light, his face red with pain and rage. "Who?"

Raven shot him through the head. Fox's big body made a pile of dead flesh stuffed in a fancy suit.

Raven pivoted. He shined the light on Ward and his wife. Mrs. Ward had reached her husband and tried to drag him behind the chair with her.

"Stop."

The couple froze in the spotlight. Ward breathed hard, straining, his leg a bloody mess.

"I'm not going to kill you, Ward. You get to live with it."

Ward forced out his response. "How did you survive?"

Raven didn't know how to answer.

"Tell me, Raven!"

Raven turned off the light and started for the door.

"Raven!"

He didn't look back.

FOUR MONTHS LATER

It was a hot summer night, but nobody complained.

Raven sat three rows back from the front in the crowded Hollywood Bowl. He watched the Los Angeles Philharmonic Orchestra. Their combined sounds filled the night. It wasn't his usual musical taste, but he wanted to see the girl at the piano. She was making a name for herself with melancholic solos. Solos which brought tears to listeners' eyes. Raven understood why. The music came from deep down, where secrets lived. The piano player was Triana Panadero.

Except it wasn't. Her legal ID said she was Alexis Santiago, from Nicaragua. She'd come to the United States to pursue a much wider career than her home country gave her. And the LA Phil fans either believed her bio without question, or didn't care. The music press tried to find out more from Ms. Santiago herself, but she didn't give interviews. She had no social media. She kept outside forces as closed off as possible.

Raven understood why, too.

After rescuing the girl from Yasmina Sevilla, Raven took her to Bogota. He settled them both at a hotel where Raven began working the phone. The DEA and CIA very much wanted to know what information about the drug trade she carried in her head. In exchange for a new life and new identity in the United States, Triana agreed to share what she knew. Because it was impossible not to have learned a lot during the years she lived as a narco's daughter.

The US government made good on its promise, and she

went to Los Angeles to try out for the LA Philharmonic. She was one of the youngest members of the orchestra. And she had the chops to keep up with the rest.

Raven sat and listened and watched Triana in the bright spotlight. She played slowly, building as the piece carried on, finally wrapping with an emotional crescendo and final lingering note. The note faded for ten seconds, in which time the audience stared in awe, then the applause began. The standing ovation followed. Raven applauded, too, and smiled. But sadness lingered behind his eyes. He was happy for her new life, but regretted the circumstances of its creation. She'd lost everything.

There were other matters on his mind, too.

How did you survive?

He wondered why Ward wanted to know. Especially while staring into a gun. More importantly, he wanted to find a suitable answer. He wanted an answer he could live with.

His thoughts turned to Dr. Gray, his daughter Kaylee, and the church missionaries. What would they tell him? But if the answer was God, it only brought to mind more questions. Why did God need Raven? Why not step in and remove the need for his war without end? The questions kept him up at night, and he was tired of wrestling with them. But maybe he didn't like the questions because he feared the answers.

It was easier not to think about them. For now, Raven only wanted a rest.

The audience sat again as the orchestra continued. They played their music long into the night.

TRIANA HAD to remember to answer to Alexis now. Sometimes, she forgot. Most of the time, her thoughts were elsewhere anyway. She wanted to get better at staying in the moment.

But it was hard. She knew her mother and father were dead because of her. If only she'd kept her mouth shut.

But what was the alternative?

Either the army would have killed them or...

It was the *or* she couldn't define. She and her mother might have survived. Her mother might have faced charges because she was as much a part of narco trafficking as...her father. Her fake father, and her real one. They were almost one and the same. But at least in prison her mother would still be alive.

She had a new name, new identity, whole new life story. Anybody who knew her old secrets was dead. The only truth was the one she gave, and she didn't talk much. She knew her orchestra colleagues wanted to know her better, but she kept them distant. She wasn't ready yet. There might be a chance she'd never be ready.

She did have a couple of friends, though. Their carpool was nice after a concert. They dropped her at the apartment she shared with two other girls her age, and entered to find she was alone. Very good. A little quiet after the noise of the concert wouldn't be unwelcome. She changed from her concert gown into sweat pants and a T-shirt.

The TV held little interest, but she flipped channels anyway.

The man who'd saved her life only gave her the name "Sam". He also said she might see "the crazy lady" in her dreams. Triana didn't think of her that way any longer. She'd learned about Yasmina Sevilla while staying with the government. But Sam wasn't wrong. She did see Yasmina in her dreams, always with a gun, always coming closer to the wrecked car. But she saw somebody else, too. Sam showed up to save her. She didn't know who he was, where he'd gone, or if she'd ever see him again. But she hoped, deep down, if the world ever turned dark again, he'd show up when she needed him most.

And if not, his presence in her dreams was enough to help her sleep when Yasmina showed up. Someday she'd be gone for good.

A LOOK AT: LONDON ASSAULT: A SAM RAVEN THRILLER

BY BRIAN DRAKE

Sam Raven is on a warpath.

MI5 suspects charity mogul Thomas Granton, a friend of King Charles, is involved with terrorists—and using his charity to fund death and destruction across the world. But they need hard proof.

Setting out to uncover the truth, complications arise when Raven discovers London's biggest crime syndicate may also be involved. As he sorts the players and identifies his targets, the enemy responds with action of their own—a surprise sleight-of-hand that points Raven in the wrong direction, resulting in a death toll he can't measure. As the stakes rise, Raven plans his all-out assault against an enemy who remains two steps ahead.

To make matters worse, the mastermind behind the conspiracy is a terrorist Raven tangled with ten years ago, and they're about to cross paths again. But this time, only one of them will walk away alive.

AVAILABLE OCTOBER 2025

ABOUT THE AUTHOR

A twenty-five year veteran of radio and television broadcasting, Brian Drake has spent his career in San Francisco where he's filled writing, producing, and reporting duties with stations such as KPIX-TV, KCBS, KQED, among many others. Currently carrying out sports and traffic reporting duties for Bloomberg 960, Brian Drake spends time between reports and carefully guarded morning and evening hours cranking out action/adventure tales.

A love of reading when he was younger inspired him to create his own stories, and he sold his first short story, "The Desperate Minutes," to an obscure webzine when he was 25 (more years ago than he cares to remember, so don't ask).

Brian Drake lives in California with his wife and two cats, and when he's not writing he is usually blasting along the back roads in his Corvette with his wife telling him not to drive so fast, but the engine is so loud he usually can't hear her.

briandrakebooks.com

www.ingramcontent.com/pod-product-compliance
Lightning Source LLC
Chambersburg PA
CBHW010827250626
47169CB00010B/2978